SIMON B. RHYMIN'

GETS IN THE GAME

SIMON B. RHYMIN'
GETS IN THE GAME

BY DWAYNE REED

ILLUSTRATED BY
ROBERT PAUL JR.

LITTLE, BROWN AND COMPANY
New York Boston

Interior design by Carla Weise.

Little, Brown and Company
Hachette Book Group
1290 Avenue of the Americas, New York, NY 10104
Visit us at LBYR.com

First Edition: April 2023

Library of Congress Cataloging-in-Publication Data
Names: Reed, Dwayne, author. | Paul, Robert, Jr., illustrator.
Title: Gets in the game / by Dwayne Reed ; illustrated by Robert Paul Jr.
Description: First edition. | New York : Little, Brown and Company, 2023. | Series: Simon B. Rhymin' ; book 3 | Audience: Ages 8–12. | Summary: When Simon joins the basketball team, he is excited to be a part of a neighborhood tradition, but after some of his teammates leave for a better team, he decides to organize a pep rally to help Creighton Park and the community feel like they are part of something special.
Identifiers: LCCN 2022036975 | ISBN 9780316441544 (hardcover) | ISBN 9780316441759 (ebook)
Subjects: CYAC: Basketball—Fiction. | Friendship—Fiction. | City and town life—Fiction. | Rap (Music)—Fiction. | African Americans—Fiction. | Chicago (Ill.)—Fiction.
Classification: LCC PZ7.1.R4278 Ge 2023 | DDC [Fic]—dc23
LC record available at https://lccn.loc.gov/2022036975

ISBNs: 978-0-316-44154-4 (hardcover),
978-0-316-44175-9 (ebook)

Printed in the United States of America

LSC-C

Printing 1, 2023

THIS ONE'S FOR ALL THE HOOPERS OUT THERE.

NEVER BE AFRAID TO TAKE THE SHOT.

MONDAY

CHAPTER 1

I LOVE CHICAGO MORE THAN ANYTHING. Low-key, Creighton Park wouldn't be the same anywhere else. Even with the ground covered in snow, like it is today, I know every crack in the sidewalk. I know which places have the best grape pop, which stores to stay away from cuz the owners are mean, and which places have the best Italian beef sandwiches. On a day like today, a sandwich like that—thin-sliced beef, just enough spice, and a bun that's been dipped in hot gravy—would be heaven.

Now, I like the winter, and the snow is pretty and everything, but every now and then we get this thing called the Polar Vortex—a swirling mass of air that comes down from way up north and makes it colder than that thang, with temperatures about ten below and wind chill even colder. On days like today, I wish our school district could be like other cities and let us stay home and watch kids pulling pranks on YouTube. But Chicago hardly ever closes the schools cuz of the weather. My older brother, Aaron, said they closed once when the snow was up to his butt, but I never got a snow day. If the snow was up to *my* butt, I'd have to trudge through it. School would be open, and there would be Mr. James, jumping on his desk to do a rap about barometric pressure or something.

It'd probably be a good rap, too. Even the Notorious D.O.G. gotta admit Mr. James got skills.

But the WORST part is we're stuck inside for recess. Which makes no sense. Sometimes the heaters don't work right, so today it's just as cold inside as outside. Maria worked hard to get us stuff like the schools on the North Side have, but I guess they ain't got around to the radiators at Booker T. Washington yet. All I know is that Polar Vortex mess ought to stay up in the North Pole, where it belong, and let us keep having recess outside, where *it* belongs.

It's the sixth straight day we have to stay inside, and nobody is happy. But I'm lookin' on the bright side: At least all the recess equipment is in here.

"Hey, fellas, I got the ball!" Maria spins the red kickball on her fingertip. She only just learned to do it, so she shows it off every chance she gets. I guess that's one good thing about having recess in the gym: no freezing-cold wind to blow the ball off her finger.

"Cool," I tell her. "You wanna go play wall ball over there?"

"We should change it up and shoot some hoops," says C.J.

Or, I think that's what he says. It's loud in the gym. In one corner a bunch of girls are jumping up and down and screaming cheers. In another, a bunch of people from Mrs. Leary's class play dodgeball with Nerf balls, only they can't keep track of who's actually playing and who's just getting too close, so a whole bunch of people are just getting hit. Out of the game before they even start playing!

"I'm not sure we can play hoops *or* wall ball," I say, looking around the gym. "All the walls and hoops already being used!"

"Then let's just toss it around," says Maria. She throws it at me, but I don't move fast enough. It goes right over my head, *whoosh*, and right into Bobby Sanchez's palm.

"You need to throw it way lower to get on Simon's level." Bobby smirks at me. Will he ever come up with new material? I'm short. We KNOW. He ain't gotta bring it up every single day.

He throws the ball and it whizzes over my head going the other way. C.J. tries to grab it but Victor G., Bobby's main sidekick, shoves into him and makes him drop it. "This is mine, loser." Then Victor shoots, and the ball goes straight through the metal hoop nearby, right in the middle of somebody's game of HORSE.

I might've been impressed if he didn't turn and look at me all smug.

I wish I didn't have to deal with Bobby and Victor *still* clowning on me all the time. I might be short on the outside, but the Notorious D.O.G. is big on the inside. One of these days Bobby and Victor are gon' put some respect on my name.

IF IT'S H...O...R...S...E
PLAYIN' WALL BALL OR SHOOTIN' REAL LONG
THREES

AROUND BOBBY SANCHEZ OR VICTOR G.
OR ANYBODY ELSE--THEY GON' NOTICE ME!
I'M SIMON THE BALLER, SIMON THE GOAT
SIMON, THE BEST ON THE COURT (I HOPE)
WELL, MAYBE NOT THE BEST, BUT I'M STILL
IN THE GAME
SO WHATEVER Y'ALL DO, JUST RESPECT MY NAME!

Someone throws the ball back, and C.J. snatches it before Victor can grab it. I run a few feet over, so this time when C.J. passes it to me I can get it. Then I turn and get in position to shoot a three-pointer. I'm wide open!

Except the hoop is looking real far away right now.

I hold up a second, and when I do, Bobby starts in.

"Bet you can't make that," he says.

He's probably right. We're back behind the three-point line, and anyway, I'm not exactly dressed for sports right now. Since it's so cold outside, Moms was all into me this morning about wearing layers. So I got on my Bulls T-shirt, the Bulls hoodie I got for Christmas, jeans, and long underwear. I didn't want to wear those long johns because that's just embarrassing, but when that wind cut through all them layers this morning, I was glad Moms made me put them on.

But now I'm standing here sweatin' in all these layers.

"Bet you he can," says C.J.

Now I'm in for it.

"Okay," says Bobby. "Let's make this interesting and bet for real."

Now I'm *really* in for it. Sometimes we tell C.J. he should speak up more, but look what happens when he does!

"I just know y'all ain't gambling," drops in Maria.

"We ain't gamblin' with money," C.J. says to her. "We gamblin' with snacks! You got a bag of Flamin' Hots for lunch?"

Bobby nods and grins. "Two of 'em."

"Aight, then. Bet."

"You're on."

Maria pushes her glasses—blue frames today—up on her nose. "That's still probably against the rules. And anyway, people are using that hoop."

"We all gotta share when we're doing indoor recess," says C.J. I can already see him getting excited about two free bags of Flamin' Hot Cheetos. I don't want to let him down or look like a fool in front of Bobby.

But I'm *really* not feelin' this three-point-line nonsense.

"I'm not sure, y'all," I say. It's hard to shoot wearing long johns.

"What are you scared of, shorty?" Bobby again. Can't he go somewhere else? Anywhere else?

Then Victor starts in. "SHORTY SIMON IS A CHICKEN! *BAWK-BOK!*"

I can see Maria getting ready to say something but I shake my head. "Ignore him!"

"WE ALL KNOW SIMON'S GONNA LOSE CUZ CHICKENS CAN'T PLAY BASKETBALL!" Victor yells, hands cupped around his mouth.

"BAWK-BOK!"

"Ain't no chickens over here!" Notorious D.O.G. ain't never scared! *Well, maybe just a little bit.*

"If Simon is the chicken, why you the one doin' all the cluckin'?" Maria is all in Bobby's face, which is turning all kinds of red. He hates when people come at him like that.

BOBBY THINKS HE'S SO TOUGH STUFF
ALL HE DOES IS HUFF AND PUFF
I WISH I WAS BRAVE ENOUGH
TO TELL HIM TO HIS FACE, "ENOUGH!"

EVERYBODY'S WATCHING US

SO EVERY WORD IS GETTING STUCK

WON'T COME OUT, WON'T COME UP

ALL OF THIS IS JUST TOO MUCH!

THEY SAYIN' THAT I'M SCARED--YUP!

CHICKEN SIMON, CLUCK CLUCK!

I JUST NEED A LITTLE LUCK

TO MAKE THE SHOT I'M 'BOUT TO CHUCK!

C.J. leans in. "You got this. And I'll get you Flamin' Hots, too, after school."

It's now or never. And if it's never I won't ever live it down. Then nobody will ever respect the Notorious D.O.G.

I close my eyes real tight and let go.

Feels like a million minutes till I hear it.

Swish!

Then: "OH EM GEE, SIMON!"

No way I made that. No way. But I did!

People are cheering like I just made the winning shot in sudden-death overtime. And C.J. is shaking my hand, all official and dramatic. "You just won yourself a bag of Flamin' Hots!"

CHAPTER 2

EVERYONE'S STILL RESTLESS AFTER THAT discount recess, carrying on when we get back to class. We *all* got some more steam to let out, plus I'm extra hype! I still can't believe I made that shot! Right in front of everybody, too. Now they gotta respect the Notorious D.O.G.!

Lil Kenny is jumping up and down at the window, seeing how high the snow's getting. It ain't much higher than it was when recess started! I kinda feel bad for Kenny today. He's one of those kids where, every recess, the first thing he does is scream at the top of his lungs and *run* all the way across the playground and back, like he's got a ton of hype to burn off before he can get down to playing. He can scream and run in the gym, but everyone knows it ain't the same.

Nobody is acting right except Maria, and she keeps looking around the class with a huffy face. "Y'all act like y'all ain't got no home training or nothing!" she yells, but nobody is listening to her.

Finally Mr. James stands up from his desk. "All right, y'all, settle down," he says. "Kenny, that's enough!"

Kenny isn't listening. Nobody is. I ain't ever seen us so rowdy, but I guess six days straight of indoor recess is taking its toll. If the Polar Vortex doesn't go back home, the whole place might explode.

Mr. James gives Kenny a serious look and raises his hand like the choir director at church directing. Then he lowers his hands, and people start to calm down. Mr. James is all right. He never yells at us. He can make the whole class calm down just by lowering his hands. It even works on Kenny two outta three times.

"Now, scholars, I understand y'all have been

cooped up inside for too long," Mr. James says. He always calls us scholars. I'm cool with it, long as he doesn't make us wear robes and those flat hats that "scholars" wear in cartoons. In fact, I like it. It makes me feel important, like I'm doing big things just by learning about fractions and stuff.

"I've got something here that might take the edge off." He holds up a piece of paper. "The Creighton Park Panthers are a coed recreational basketball team, and we're recruiting for this season's league. Everybody gets a chance to play at every game. And the best part? You don't even have to try out. Just sign up and show out."

I sit up real straight when I hear that.

The Panthers!

Creighton Park Panthers have been part of Creighton since before even Dad and Moms were little. Mr. Ray, the barber, has a bunch of pictures of the team from back in the day, when it was all boys and half of them had those old-fashioned-type Afros, the kind that look like cotton balls, not the kind people have now. I guess they were one of the top rec teams in the city. Now they ain't so good. Mr. Ray is always talking about how they barely won a game the last four seasons.

But I don't care. All three of my brothers played on the team. So it's a family tradition. And after that shot I just made, I'm feelin' pretty good. Maybe I can even help the Panthers have a decent season!

THE NEW ADDITION TO THE PANTHERS IS ME!
SIMON BARNES, NOTORIOUS D.O.G.!
THE THREE-POINT-MAKER, THE QUICK
FAST-BREAKER,
THE SMOOTH PUMP-FAKER, THE BIG
SHOT-TAKER!
KEEPING THE TRADITION OF THE FAM GOIN'

STRONG
CUZ NOT BEING A PANTHER WOULD BE SO WRONG!
SO I'M GONNA BE ON THE TEAM THIS YEAR
AND FILL EVERY OTHER TEAM WITH CREIGHTON
PARK FEAR!
WOOF WOOF!

"How much it cost?" Kenny asks. For once I'm glad he's speakin' out of turn. He can't be the only one wondering.

"All free," Mr. James says. "We got your uniforms. We got a coach. And you got me as assistant coach. We got the community center. You just need to be ready to play."

"What you know about assistant coaching?" asks Kenny.

"Join the team and you'll see."

"I'm in," Bobby says. "This neighborhood *needs* me."

For the hundredth time today, I start sweatin' under my arms. Playing on the Panthers won't be as much fun if Bobby is there, but I can't punk out now. Aaron and DeShawn and Markus won't ever let me live it down. *I* won't let me live it down.

"Sign me up, too," I say.

Bobby breaks out laughing. "Shorty Simon playing on a team?"

"You saw him make that shot!" says Maria.

"Sure, he made a three-pointer just standing there, but it's different in a game!" says Bobby. "He gon' have people a foot taller blocking him!"

"Not all basketball players are tall," says Mr. James. "Spud Webb was five foot *seven*. That's eleven inches shorter than Michael Jordan. And he won the slam-dunk contest the year I was born."

"Really?" I ask.

"Ha!" Bobby laughs. "Only way Simon's ever slam-dunking is if he cuts one so hard he lifts off the ground!"

I try to give Bobby a dirty look, but honestly even I have to laugh at that one. Everyone does, and Mr. James does the thing with his hands. He always says scholars don't make jokes about people cutting one. But it's a losing battle; sooner or later, someone *does* cut one, every day, and then we all bust up laughin'.

"There's more to basketball than slam dunks, scholars," says Mr. James. "It's a mental game, just as much as a physical one. The best players play smart, not just tall." He passes me the clipboard with the sign-up sheet.

I'm really nervous now. But it's a family tradition, and Notorious D.O.G. needs to step up. Don't matter if Bobby Sanchez will be trying to harsh my vibe.

I put down my name.

CHAPTER 3

MARIA AND I WALK HOME FROM SCHOOL with Ms. Estelle. Some days Ms. Estelle talks just as much as Maria, but today she's all bundled up in about a hundred scarves, so it's hard to hear her. Much of what she does say is in Spanish. Every gust of wind, she says, "Ay Dios mío!" which I know is Spanish for "OH EM GEE!"

C.J. is with us so we can settle up our bet. While we walk, I kick at the snow on the ground. There's a good two inches of new stuff, but it's all just ice and powder.

Maria can't stop talking about the three-pointer.

"I still can't believe you did that, Simon! And you did it with your eyes closed. That's even better!"

"What if eyes closed is the only way I can do it?"

"So?" C.J. asks. "Nobody care *how* it's done, just that you *got* it done. Even if you did look constipated."

"Like you been stopped up for three weeks," Maria adds.

"Very funny."

We stop when we get to Wheeler's Corner Store. The building is real old, with crumbling bricks and faded painted signs from places that don't exist anymore. Dad says they're called ghost signs and they're all over the city. One of them on the side of the wall at Wheeler's is so faded you can't read much of it, but two of the words you can make out are *Delivery Wagons*. Like from back before there were even cars!

I like going there. They have candy and pop that you can't get a lot of places anymore. I'm in the mood for a bottle of Duck Island Concord Grape, the best grape pop anywhere on the planet. Usually C.J. gets two Flamin' Hots for a buck, but since I won the bet, he'll give me the second one.

"You gonna sign up for the Panthers, or what?" I ask C.J.

"I dunno," he says. "I'm not that good, really."

"Don't have to be for rec league!"

"And I got other stuff to do, too," he says.

"Like what?" asks Maria. "Cartoon Network marathons?"

"Of course! You only get one childhood, right? Gotta make the most of it."

Some people might say playing basketball is making the most of your childhood, not watching cartoons you've already seen a hundred times. But that's C.J. for ya. Plus, I bet he's worried the coach will tell him to lay off the snacks. That'd be a deal-breaker for C.J.

"Well, how come *you* ain't signed up?" I ask Maria. "Bet nobody else can spin a ball like you."

"I got debate team," she says. "And I'm gonna debate you right into joining up, C.J."

I don't know why it bugs Maria that C.J. doesn't sign up for more stuff, but it does. I think she just wants him to get involved rather than watch cartoons.

The bell on the door rings as we walk into the

store, and Mr. Wheeler smiles. Mr. Ray, the barber next door, is behind the counter with him. Sometimes when Mr. Ray doesn't have any hair to cut, he goes over to the store so they can drink coffee and talk about the news or whatever.

"Here comes Rhymin' Simon!" Mr. Wheeler says. Everyone in the neighborhood knows I'm always rhymin'. But I think he might have been the first to call me that, except my brother DeShawn, who made it up. I do know that when I was just a shorty, I came into Wheeler's with Moms one time and said, "I would like a piece of gum, I think chewing would be fun."

It wasn't a very good rhyme, but I remember for sure Mr. Wheeler called me Rhymin' Simon that day.

I guess the Notorious D.O.G. was born to rhyme.

"How's it going?" I ask.

Maria and her grandmother go to the back to start looking over the flavored sticks of hard candy, which Maria says are the best value for your money. I got a buck, so I start looking in the little cooler, but I don't see the grape pop I like.

"Hey, Mr. Wheeler," I say. "Are you out of the Duck Island Concord Grape?"

"'Fraid so," he says. "Ain't been able to stock back up yet."

I'm just trying to pick something else when C.J. says, "Hey! What gives?"

"Something wrong?" asks Mr. Wheeler.

"The Flamin' Hots are sixty cents now?"

Mr. Wheeler nods, even though he looks kinda sad. "Had to get the prices up a bit."

"I can't get two for a dollar now!" says C.J. I

know he mad. Now he can only get one bag, and he gotta give it to me.

I decide not to get a drink; it's too cold anyway. Who wants a cold drink when there's a Polar Vortex blowing around?

We go back to where Maria is looking at the candy sticks.

"I bet they didn't raise the price at the Kwik Spot," C.J. mutters.

"What's Kwik Spot?" I ask.

"A new store right by my house. Just opened last week. I ain't been in it yet, but my dad loves it. Says they got it all in there, and cheap."

Thinking about going to a corner store that's not Wheeler's don't sit right with me. It makes my stomach feel weird. I don't care even if that new place might have the Concord Grape.

Back at the register, I can hear Mr. Ray and Mr. Wheeler talking.

"I don't know," Mr. Wheeler is saying. "Ever since Kwik Spot opened, it's been real slow. Hardly anybody coming in."

"Ain't nothin' good ever coming when those places open up around here." Mr. Ray shakes his head. "Say, you think you gon' get in some more hot pickles? Like in the next two minutes?"

Mr. Wheeler rubs his balding head. "Gotta see how the rest of the month goes."

"No pickles?" Maria asks. She likes to stick a peppermint stick into a pickle sometimes. I think it's nasty, but she says it's a neighborhood classic. I'll take her word for it.

But we look at each other a second. This is the only store in town with good hot pickles. If Wheeler's stops carrying them, a lotta people gon' be upset.

C.J. figures out that he can still get one of the hard candy sticks plus the Flamin' Hots bag he owes me, so he picks out a cinnamon one. Not quite the same, but close enough.

When we bring our stuff up to the counter, Mr. Wheeler looks me up and down. "I swear, Rhymin' Simon, you get taller every time I see you."

"I know that's right," Mr. Ray says. "Like weeds! Where the time goin'? Cuz I know I'm not the one getting older. Me and the Lord were supposed to have a deal!"

I stand up straighter while Mr. Ray and Mr. Wheeler laugh. Maybe I am growing a little bit. I hope so. No matter what Mr. James says about Spud Webb, everyone knows it helps to be tall if you play basketball. And I'm a Panther now.

THIS TRIP TO THE STORE IS NOT GOIN' REAL GREAT!
THERE'S NO PICKLES FOR MARIA, OR NO
 CONCORD GRAPE!
ALL THE PRICES GOIN' ON UP, ALL THE WAY TO
 THE TOP
PLUS, I HEAR THERE'S ANOTHER STORE CALLED
 KWIK SPOT.

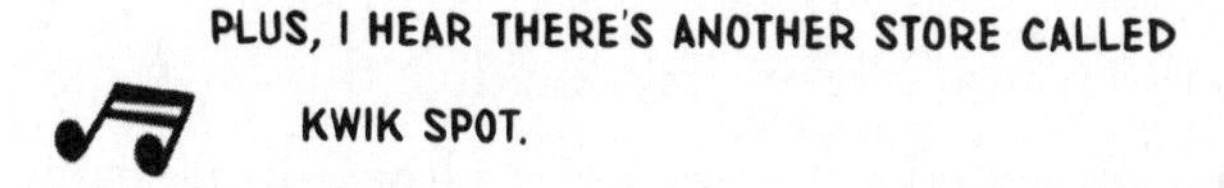

THEY GOT REAL LOW PRICES, EVERYTHING'S
 REAL CHEAP.
AND I BET THEY GOT EVERYTHING A KID
 WANTS TO EAT
BUT I LOVE MR. WHEELER'S, SO IT'S MAKING
 ME SAD
THAT HE DON'T GOT THE STUFF THAT HE
 USUALLY HAS.

WHY GO SOMEWHERE ELSE IF THIS PLACE
HERE'S FINE?
HE'LL GET WHAT HE NEEDS, HE JUST NEEDS
MORE TIME.
WHY GO SOMEWHERE ELSE IF THIS PLACE
HERE'S FINE?
HE'LL GET WHAT HE NEEDS, HE JUST NEEDS
MORE TIME.

Mr. Wheeler rings up C.J.'s stuff with a giant old-fashioned cash register. It's bronze-colored and has a lot of patterns carved in the metal. The price doesn't come up on a screen. It pops up with these different-colored flag-looking things. I like the sounds it makes. It don't beep like normal cash registers. Instead it makes all kinds of thumping and clanking noises, and it says *cha-ching* when the drawer pops out. I think it's real neat and got a lot more personality than the scanners at Target that just go *beep beep beep*. I can hear a beep anyplace.

When he rings us up, Mr. Wheeler looks at me. "Nothing for you today, Simon?"

"C.J. owes me his Flamin' Hots."

"Now, I know you're not gambling, right?"

"Not for money! Just for snacks."

He shakes his head and says something about how it's still not smart, cuz it takes money to buy snacks anyway. "That's what I said!" Maria says.

Her grandmother mutters something in Spanish, only I don't know what it means. Probably something about how gambling is wrong. Or how she hit it big in Vegas back in the day.

Wheeler reaches into a jar and pulls up one of those pieces of bubble gum that come in red-and-blue paper wrappers. "So let's call this a deal, not a bet," he says. "Free piece of gum if you give me a good rhyme."

That's another thing that never happen at Target. Even the checkers who've known us forever don't give us gum for rapping.

And I'm a lot better than I was back when I was little.

"Bubble gum, red and blue. Give me a piece and I gotta chew. Blowing bubbles big and round, till Concord Grape comes back to town!"

He smiles and hands me the gum.

Half the time I don't know where I even come up with this stuff. Just what the Notorious D.O.G. was born to do.

But as we step out of the store, I see this shadow in Mr. Wheeler's eyes. And just like that, my stomach feels all messed up again.

Something seems like it's going wrong with Mr. Wheeler's store. Maybe it's just that people don't buy many snacks when the wind chill is below zero. I look up at the wall of the building. Through the snow, I see just a bit of the old DELIVERY WAGONS sign.

Whatever business sold delivery wagons is long gone. Nothing left but a faded old sign on the building.

Wheeler's place couldn't end up like that. Could it?

CHAPTER 4

MY APARTMENT BUILDING, CREIGHTON Crest, is gonna be a hundred years old pretty soon. From the outside it looks like a redbrick cube, four apartments on each of the four floors. Looking out the window of the bedroom I share with my brothers—or what I see of it through all the stuff Markus and DeShawn got piled in front of it—I can see all these old houses across the street that musta been pretty fancy when they was built. They aren't mansions, like the kind you see on TV, and they don't have a yard like C.J.'s, but they got towers and columns and even faces carved into the stone on a couple of 'em. Dad says when they were built they used to be single-family houses, but now they're all broken up into apartments. But Creighton Crest was always apartments.

Sometimes I look at those old houses and wonder how many other people sat at this same window and wondered what the *Crest* in *Creighton Crest* meant. Probably a lot. Maybe some of the first Panthers lived in this same apartment. Maybe people who were in those pictures of marches we saw during our social studies lessons.

But I *know* ain't none of them got to smell anything as good as the smell that was coming in my room before dinner.

It's like Dad read my mind about how good an Italian beef sandwich would taste, because that's what he made! In other cities, most sandwich places never even heard of Italian beef, which is one more reason you can't beat Chicago. But Dad's recipe is the best in town, and he always makes homemade mac and cheese on the side. Most places with sandwiches, you get fries or chips. Hot Italian beef sandwiches and mac and cheese are a Barnes family thing.

Just like the Panthers, in a way.

And best of all, I know Dad probably got most of the ingredients at Wheeler's, so that makes me feel better. Most of the year there's at least one thing on the table from the community garden where Moms grows vegetables and stuff, but nothing grows in a Polar Vortex, I don't think.

"I'm gonna need the biggest sandwich you got," I say as I sit down.

"Huh-uh!" says Aaron. "I have permanent dibs on the biggest. I'm a growing boy." He is always saying stuff like that now that he's in high school.

Markus and DeShawn, who are in middle school, come into the kitchen behind Aaron, ready to fight him on that.

"I'm growing faster," says Markus. "Once you get up in high school, you done growing. Just growing *out* from here!"

"Better just hope your hair keep growing," says DeShawn. "I think you're about old enough that it might start falling out."

They always clown on him for being old, like he as old as the building.

"Well, I need to do some growing," I say. "I signed up for the Panthers today!"

Aaron stops scrolling on his phone and looks up. "For real?"

Dad takes out one of his AirPods. He always listens to podcasts while he's cooking.

"Did I hear that right?" he asks as he sits down. "You signed up for basketball?"

I nod and start piling a bunch of beef into my sandwich.

"You hear that?" asks Dad as Moms walks by to change out of her work clothes. "The tradition of Barnes boys in the Panthers continues!"

"Wonderful," says Moms. "Get me the schedule when you can, so I can try to arrange work around the games."

"That's dope, man!" says Markus. "Shortest person ever in the league! Let's go!"

"Short people can hoop," I say. "Ain't you ever heard of Spud Webb?"

"He was still taller than *you*," says Markus.

"You should have seen me at recess today," I say. "Bobby and C.J. had a bet that I couldn't make a three-pointer. I had everyone looking at me, and *SWISH!* Nothing but net."

Aaron nods. "I was the best scorer on the Panthers when I was your age," he says. "And that's the last time they had a winning team. Maybe we can shoot a few hoops this weekend, if it's not too cold."

I'm so surprised I almost let him take most of the Italian beef for his sandwich. Me, DeShawn, Markus, and him are tight. Always have been. But ever since he got to high school, Aaron's been acting like he's all grown and the rest of us are just little kids. When we went to get signatures for Maria's petition to save the school clubs and Moms made him take us, he acted like it was the end of the world or something. Maybe now that I'm a Panther, he'll like it better. Dope.

I take my first bite, and it's everything I hoped it would be. All the cold that was left in my insides from walking home just starts to melt. Like, I feel it burning up inside me, but in a good way. Some of the gravy dribbles down my chin.

After a few bites, I ask, "You get all this stuff at Wheeler's?"

"The buns and the noodles, sure," says Dad. "The meat and cheese, I had to go to the big grocery store. They don't have that stuff at Wheeler's much."

"Used to, back in the day," says Moms.

"Wasn't the best place to go for meat, even then," says Dad. "But you can't get hot pickles at the big grocery store."

"Can't at Wheeler's right now, either," I say. "He ran out! All out of my Concord Grape, too. He and Mr. Ray were talking in there. Prices have to go up."

Moms and Dad look at each other a minute, like they're worried about something, but then Dad just smiles and says, "Well, now that you're a Panther, we'll have to get you more snacks, too, wherever we have to go to get them."

I think I'ma like being a Panther!

TUESDAY

CHAPTER 5

AT RECESS, C.J. IS LEANING BACK, INHALING, and smiling. "Dreaming about nuggets," he says. At Booker T. Washington Elementary, the gym is also the cafeteria and auditorium. So gym class always kinda smells like chicken nuggets. And since it's still too cold to go outside, so does recess. (Weird thing is: The place smells like chicken nuggets no matter what's for lunch.)

C.J. has the same look on his face that his dad gets listening to jazz music. C.J.'s teachers always say the same thing: He lives in his own little world. He has to doodle a lot to stay focused. Sometimes when you talk to him, he looks like he's not even listening, but then he can repeat back everything you just said, like his brain is in two places at once. And he always gets good grades. His dad says people just got different learning styles. Because of that, he sits in the back row and gets some kinda deal where they don't stop him doodling all the time, long as he gets his work done. For a while, before his dad came in and talked to some teachers, he was getting in trouble for it. But when he can't doodle to stay focused, he gets lost. His grades go way down. When they let him work the way that fits his brain, they go back up.

Actually, I think he's kinda like Lil Kenny in a way. Like, his brain gets so pent up that it wants to go running and screaming first chance it can.

I didn't make it to the gym in time to grab a ball this recess, and neither did C.J. or Maria, so we kind of hang out on the edges, hoping something will turn up and wishing we were outside.

"At least you'll get to play *when* you sign up for the Panthers," Maria tells C.J. She's been trying all day to get him to join.

"I dunno," he say. "Coaches yell a lot, right?"

"Mr. James ain't the yelling kind," I say. "I know you got game, too. The Panthers need you."

"I got games to play at home," he says. "And TV to watch. And no one makes me run laps or eat lettuce. Last night I saw a basketball player on TV talking 'bout how he has to eat raw kale and drink apple cider vinegar. You think I wanna drink vinegar just to play basketball?"

"It's just a rec league," I say. "No one's gonna make you give up Flamin' Hots to play rec basketball."

"Still might make me run laps, though."

I don't think we'll have to do all that boring stuff. C.J. just don't know cuz he's in Mrs. Leary's class. I can't picture Mr. James blowing a whistle and telling us to run laps. That's not his style. Anyway, he says basketball is a mental game. He'll probably just make us sit and think. Even C.J. can handle that kinda thing.

Maybe I should be running laps right now. Gotta get in shape for the team if I want us to win any games this year.

"Speaking of Flamin' Hots," C.J. says. "My dad

took me and Deijah to Kwik Spot last night, and they got more snacks than at Five Below. And it's cheap! Their potato chips are still two for a dollar. Clerk told me sometimes they go on sale *three* for a buck."

"That's a good deal," I say.

"My dad says Wheeler's place is all overpriced, falling apart, and out of date," he says. "Can't even get meat or fresh veggies there anymore half the time." Then he stops a second and says, "I mean, if you like fresh veggies."

"They got those at Kwik Spot?" asks Maria.

"Well, no, it's still just snacks. But it's more, and it's cheaper, and they got all the new equipment. And no one there's gonna waste my time telling me how much I've grown."

All the while we're talking, Maria has been fiddling with her glasses—pink frames today—looking like she's thinking hard about something. But there's no test coming up today.

Finally, she says, "My sister went to Kwik Spot the other day. Says the same thing, pretty much. They got a lot of snacks."

"I guess I'm down to check it out," I say. "Where there's snacks, there's the Notorious D.O.G."

"Well, she says it has a lot, but it's all...you know. People in uniforms. Big-business stuff. She says it's bad for the community."

"Yeah," I say, "but your sister also says gym shoes are uncomfortable, so what she know?"

"She doesn't say they're not comfy, she says they overpriced, consumeristic, capitalistic traps to keep people down."

"Same thing, right?"

"Not really."

Maria's sister, Camille, is in middle school now. And ever since she got there, she's been all into that political stuff. In the fall we did petitions and some protests to try to save the debate team, so I know a bit about how all that stuff works. But the stuff Camille says? Right over my head. I wonder if Maria will be just like her in middle school? Or if I will?

Maria fiddles with her glasses some more and says, "She did say they got a lot of ice cream there. Like, all different brands."

"You and your ice cream. I'm surprised you just don't eat the snow off the ground and call it *winter flavor*." Oh man, I can picture her doing it! Like, scoop a handful of snow off a fire hydrant and say, "Ah, the taste of Chicago winter."

She wrinkles her nose at me. "You know darn well it's unsanitary to eat *anything* off the ground."

Speaking of gym shoes, I look down at C.J.'s. His gym shoes have seen better days. They're all scuffed up and probably don't have any traction left. It's a wonder he don't slip on the ice when we're walking to school. Half the time I wish I had cleats on myself.

"You know," I say, "I bet if you joined the Panthers, your dad would have to get you new shoes."

He brightens right up at that. "You think so?"

"Let me see under your shoe."

He lifts his foot up, and I'm right. All the treads are worn down.

"Yep," I say. "No traction. He ain't gonna want you slipping and sliding on your butt all the way up and down the court."

"I'm outgrowing them anyway," C.J. says. "Dad's just been trying to hold out as long as he can, waiting till he thinks I *really* need a new pair. Like, when my toes poke out the front."

"You go one more day without taking a bath and the stink off your feet's gonna make those shoes shrivel up and rot," says Maria. "I swear, I smell 'em already!"

C.J. nods. I can tell he's thinking about it.

And I know he's good at basketball. I've seen him shoot baskets a million times. Like, he's never been much for one-on-one, cuz he likes games where you stand still better, but when we're playing PIG or something, he wins every time. He woulda made that three-pointer, no problem. With him *and* the Notorious D.O.G. on the Panthers, I bet we could honestly own that court!

I start picturing us out there, doing no-look passes and dribbling between our legs, and all the people on the other teams so impressed that all they can do is stand there. I only got okayyy skills, but I got smarts and speed. He has okayyy smarts and speed, and better skills. Put us together and *bam!* Everybody gotta watch out—cuz here come the Panthers!

BASKETBALL FANS, GATHER ROUND AND LISTEN.
THE NEW PANTHER PAIR IS HERE ON A MISSION.
THE BEST TAG TEAM SINCE JORDAN AND PIPPEN.
IT'S C.J. AND SIMON, WON'T CATCH US SLIPPIN'
BUT YOU'LL SEE US DRIBBLIN', UP AND DOWN
THE COURT.

I CAN DO TONS OF MOVES, EVEN THOUGH
I'M SHORT.
I CAN PASS LIKE MAGIC, I CAN SHOOT LIKE
STEPH,
AND C.J. CAN DO IT ALL, HE'S TRULY THE BEST!
DID YOU SEE THAT CROSSOVER? HE'S LIKE
D-ROSE!
AND THAT FADEAWAY SHOT? THAT WAS JUST
TOO COLD!

IF YOU SEE US IN THE GAME, BETTA WATCH THE
SCORE
CUZ S. BARNES AND C. JONES ARE GONNA RIP
AND ROAR!

CHAPTER 6

AFTER SCHOOL, C.J. COMES UP TO ME. "All right. I'll check out the first practice. But if I don't like it, I'm leaving."

"Bet."

When we get to the basketball court at the rec center, some people are already there but I only recognize a few of them, like this girl Janay, who was in my class last year. She's kinda clumsy, but she's super tall. Kinda reminds me of Kenny, since she never takes anything serious, and she don't mind acting a fool to be the center of attention.

Victor and Bobby are standing under the basket,

holding up the ball. "Yo, C.J.! Two-on-two?" C.J. daps me up, and we run out onto the gym floor. He must be thinking of joining, or he probably wouldn't even be down for two-on-two!

Once we start up, C.J. steals the ball, dribbles, then passes it over to me. I go for the shot, but Bobby blocks me.

"Ha!" he says. "I'm gonna have to do *all* the work on the Panthers."

When I get the ball again, I take another shot, and it barely hits the rim. But C.J. grabs it for the rebound—backwards!—and shoots it up. *Swish!*

Even Victor says, "Whoa."

"That's some mighty good shootin'." Mr. James stands there, fiddling with the whistle around his neck. I was so into the game I didn't even see him come in. Next to him is a lady with a whistle of her own. She looks like an older version of Janay. I wonder if it's her moms. But just when I'm trying to get a ball to start warming up, too, she blows the whistle and shouts out, "Gather up, Panthers!"

I love hearing her say "Panthers" and knowing she means ME. The Notorious D.O.G. is a Panther

PANTHERS
1

now, just like my brothers before me. It's weird, but it makes me feel almost...powerful. The kind of way I usually only feel when I bust out some dope rhymes. As we gather up, it's almost like I feel at the Community Open Mics. Like I'm a part of something big.

"All right, Panthers!" shouts the woman. "I'm Coach Thomas."

"And I'm Assistant Coach James," says Mr. James.

She gives him a look, like he's not supposed to be the one talking right now, then starts us off introducing ourselves. I was right about her being Janay's mom. She nods to Janay first, and Janay says, "You know me, Mom."

"I'm not Mom here, I'm Coach Thomas. And your name is?"

"Janay. And when we getting the pretzels?"

"I told you. After practice, *if* you work hard."

Coach nods over to me, and I break out a rhyme: "I'm Simon B. Shootin' Threes!"

Besides me, C.J., Bobby, and Victor, there's a few other kids I don't know too well but recognize from around Booker T. One of them, Levon, was in my class in kindergarten, but I mostly remember that the teacher was always having to stop him from eating glue. I hope he's not doing that no more. Ha!

Once Coach gets through us all, Mr. James says, "I want everyone to know, first of all, that basketball isn't just running around or about being tall. It's a mental game."

"But," says Coach Thomas, "what we're going to focus on here is fundamentals. Anyone know what that means?"

"It comes from the word *fundament*," says Mr. James, "which means 'foundation.'"

He does this sometimes. He likes to show us how you take English words apart, and how you can see bits of the old French and Roman and even African words that they came from. He also says it's really high school stuff, but he thinks that, as scholars, we should get a jump on it.

But Coach Thomas gives him a look. "That's about right," she says. "Foundation. The basics. Dribbling. Shooting. Running. All the stuff you need to know to play some basketball without hurting yourself or looking like a fool. And I wasn't going for the Greek root word or whatever."

"It's Latin," says Mr. James.

"I know that. And *fundament* is an old-fashioned word for your butt, too."

We all laugh, like we always do when someone brings up butts.

Coach says, "I was going for the first part of the word: FUN. We are here to have FUN. We gotta work if we're all gonna get better at basketball and win a few games, but the number one thing here is FUN-damentals. Coach James, will you bring in the water bottles?"

It's kinda fun seeing him get bossed around! He don't seem to mind, though. He just heads off to get the water.

"Get the pretzels while you're at it!" Janay shouts.

Coach Thomas ignores her and breaks us up into pairs. She has us warm up by just dribbling and passing the balls back and forth. The basketballs are kinda worn down, all smooth with no grip, and if they were ever orange, they aren't anymore.

They're brown and kinda leathery. They must be ancient. But just think: Maybe they're so old that Isaiah Thomas or Patrick Beverley used this exact ball I'm using now! Everyone knows they're from the West Side, just like me.

My dribbling ain't great. I bounce the ball off my feet a couple times. I gotta say, this ain't a good start. C.J. keeps missing passes cuz he's distracted, watching other people or looking up at something on the ceiling. I'm afraid he's gonna be a disaster. He might have some skills, but I can't tell if he's gonna use them or what.

But once Coach Thomas breaks us into two teams to start playing a little—scrimmaging she calls it—it's like C.J. switches completely. Like he goes from being Bruce Wayne right into Batman. He's stealing the ball, he's making every shot, he's jumping higher than I thought he even could. When I try to dribble under my leg it bounces off my knee, but C.J. goes behind his back and everything! He's playing almost like a pro!

Much as I hate to say it, Victor and Bobby are good. They make most of the shots they take, they play good defense. At least against me. I go for one shot and Bobby swats it down hard. For once I don't mind him acting all tough. We're on the same team, right? If he's this tough on me, I know he'll be even tougher when we start playing other teams on Fridays.

Bobby's cousin Louis is on the team, too. He's not quite as good as Bobby, but he's what Coach Thomas calls consistent. Not flashy, but you can count on him when it comes to fundamentals.

I woulda thought Janay was just here for the pretzels. She yells about them every chance she can find. But on the court, she's even tougher than Bobby. You gotta watch out for her elbows. She makes some awesome shots but misses a couple easy ones.

A couple of the other kids act like they ain't taking this seriously. Like their parents just signed them up to get them out of the house. Coach Thomas keeps having to blow the whistle to get them to stop playing hot hands and stuff.

She does shout, but it's all good stuff. She doesn't yell at us when we make mistakes, she mostly just yells out tips.

Mr. James yells out quotes. He really loves quotes and he's got a million of 'em. Things like "Give a hundred and ten percent," "There's no *I* in *TEAM*," and "Failing to prepare is preparing to fail." Stuff I've already heard a million times before.

There's no question who the worst player is, though: That would be me. It seems like half the time I try to dribble it bounces off my foot. Victor and Bobby keep saying I must wear a size 78 in gym shoes.

I try to keep from dribbling so much, but then I end up getting called for traveling. And when I try to steal the rock, people just toss the ball right over my head. I can't reach! Basketball might be a mental game, but being a few inches taller would help a TON.

And that three-pointer I made yesterday must have been pure luck, because this time I can't make a shot. A couple come close, and a few times they bounce off the rim so C.J. can grab the rebound, but nothing I shoot goes in.

Some of Coach Thomas's tips about how to stand and all seem like they're helping, but it's pretty clear that my whole fantasy about running the court was just that: a fantasy. I'm more likely to fall on my fundament in front of everybody.

But it's all still fun. I get to be a Panther, and with C.J. and Bobby around, we still got a good chance of winning a game or two. I bet there's short kids on the other rec league teams, too. It doesn't even bother me much that I stink worse than my brothers' socks.

At least, not until the end, when Coach Thomas has us all working on free throws. C.J. makes both of his shots. So does Bobby. Most other kids make one out of two.

And then last up: me.

All right, I tell myself. Everybody watching. I can show them I *do* got game. Just like back in the gym at recess.

I set the ball like Coach Thomas says, aim, and shoot. It bounces off the backboard, hits the rim, then bounces to the ground. So close!

Louis reaches in and passes it back to me so I can take the second shot.

This is it.

READY...AIM...SHOOT THE BALL.
WILL IT GO INTO THE HOOP, OR FALL?
LAST SHOT WAS BAD, IT CLANGED ALL AROUND
OFF THE BACKBOARD TILL IT HIT THE GROUND.
THIS IS FREE THROW? DON'T FEEL SO FREE!
EVERYBODY ON THE TEAM'S GOT SKILLS
BUT ME!

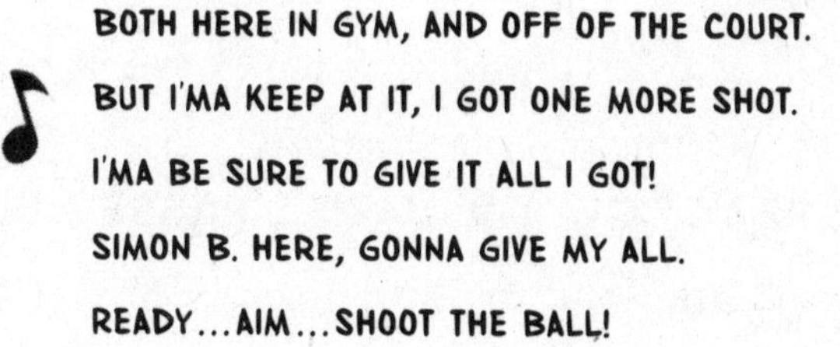

EVEN THOUGH I WORK HARD, I STILL COME
UP SHORT
BOTH HERE IN GYM, AND OFF OF THE COURT.
BUT I'MA KEEP AT IT, I GOT ONE MORE SHOT.
I'MA BE SURE TO GIVE IT ALL I GOT!
SIMON B. HERE, GONNA GIVE MY ALL.
READY...AIM...SHOOT THE BALL!

Only, it turns out, this is NOT it.

I take the shot, and it lands on the ground. Doesn't even hit the rim or the backboard.

Bobby and Victor and Louis and Janay and even a couple of the other kids—heck, I think everyone but C.J.—start going "Aiiiiirrr ball. Aiiirrrrr ball."

Okay, this part isn't so much fun.

This Panthers stuff is a lot harder than I thought it was gonna be.

CHAPTER 7

AFTER PRACTICE, MR. JAMES PASSES OUT the water bottles and the little packets of pretzels Janay was so excited about. I wanna see what the big deal is, but it's hard to taste anything when *aiiiiirrr ball* keeps playing in my mind.

When Mr. James finishes passing out the pretzels, he comes over to C.J., clipboard in hand. "You were mighty impressive out there, young man."

C.J. ducks his head, all shy and stuff.

"You're signing up, right?" Mr. James asks.

"You sure it don't cost nothing?"

Mr. James nods.

"And you won't make me give up Flamin' Hots?"

"Those are about as healthy as eating toxic sludge, but I promise not to make you give them up for basketball. Can't promise the head coach won't, but I'll put in a word."

"Think you can tell my dad I need new shoes?"

Mr. James looks down at C.J.'s feet. "I don't want to tell your dad what to do," he says. "But those don't look totally safe. If he can't get you a pair, we'll see what we can work out."

C.J. smiles. "Where do I sign?"

Once C.J. is officially a Panther, Coach Thomas has us gather around. She tells us that after the next practice we have to pick out a captain for the team. Aaron was captain when he was in the Panthers. I knew it was a long shot for me, but before practice, I thought maybe I had a chance.

Ain't no one gon' vote for Air Ball Barnes, though.

Coach starts assigning positions. "We're not going to stick with these the whole season," she says. "I want everybody to mix it up and try new things. Sometimes it may not work. But we don't have to win to represent Creighton Park. We just have to show up and do our best, try new things, and have a good time doing it. You think you can all do that?"

We all cheer, even though I'm kinda doubting it right about now. I don't know if bouncing basketballs off my feet is the best way to represent my hood, feel me? Trying new things, having a good time, all that is aight, but I don't want people thinking Creighton is a complete mess, like I am out there.

"Simon," she says, "at the next practice, we're going to work on you as point guard."

I'm shocked. "Point guard?"

"The point guard sets the tempo, controls the offense, and gets the ball to the right people. It's important."

I'm not totally sure what *tempo* means, but I nod.

"Shorty Simon on point guard? We're dead meat," says Bobby.

"They're gonna kick our fundaments," says Victor.

Coach Thomas gives them the kind of death glare that Mr. James never gives nobody. "Muggsy

Bogues was a point guard," she says. "He was five three. Lot of guys he was playing against were two feet taller. Simon may be short, but ain't one of you two feet taller than him."

"But I'm bouncing the ball off my feet half the time!" I say. "Don't point guards have to be able to dribble?"

"We'll work on that," she says. "We gonna work on all the fundamentals and figure out how to do the best with what we got."

"And giving a hundred and ten percent," says Mr. James.

She says C.J. is gonna be power forward, which I can tell bugs Bobby and Victor. They probably wanted that position for themselves. But they get put at small forward and center. Janay is gonna be the other guard. Anyway, like Coach said, it's just for now. We'll switch up soon.

But for now, I just keep hearing it in my head.

Aiiiiirrrr balll.

Aiirrrr ball.

CHAPTER 8

"Y'ALL AIN'T TOO OLD TO RUB ELBOWS."

That's what C.J.'s dad, who I call Uncle Jamaal even though he's not really my uncle, says every time he gives us all a ride in his pickup truck. He's a painter and handyman, but I guess not many people get stuff painted when it's this cold, cuz he has the afternoon off and comes to give us a ride home.

C.J. sits right by his dad in the middle seat, and Maria and I cram into the passenger seat. As we drive off, he's got old jazz music blasting so loud I can hardly hear C.J. telling him about the Panthers. He likes that far-out kind of jazz music that goes superfast. Maria whispers in my ear that it sounds like whoever's playing the saxophone is having a temper tantrum. I try to whisper back that to me it sounds like he has to pee, so he's trying to play all the notes as fast as he can and get it over with so he can dash off to the bathroom.

But while they're talking, Uncle Jamaal is just grooving along, drumming on the steering wheel. He says music like this can take you to whole new worlds. But sometimes I think he and C.J. are both already *living* in some whole other world.

Anyway, I kinda dig the music. It's keeping me from thinking about other stuff.

"How was practice for you?" Maria asks me.

My face gets hot. "I guess I'm more cut out to be a rapper, not a basketball star."

"But I saw you make that three-pointer yesterday."

"Yeah, but this time the ball didn't even make it to the backboard."

"OH EM GEEEE!" she says. "Did people start doing that thing where they all go 'Aiiiirr balll'?"

"Don't remind me."

"But that's *magic,*" she says.

"How you figure clowning on somebody is magic?"

"My grandmother sings in the choir at church. She says the hardest thing is learning to all start singing at the same time."

"So?"

"And even in the choir, half the people have trouble hitting the right notes. It takes a lot of practice."

"So?"

"So, when there's an air ball, everyone all starts chanting at once, without even having a choir director to tell them. And they always sing it right on pitch, too! *Aiiirr*—that's an F note. Then *ballll.* D note. Everyone magically has perfect pitch and sings on cue!"

That's one way to look at it, I guess. But I sure wish I coulda made magic by doing something *good.* And I wish they used that magic for something better than clowning on me.

Uncle Jamaal drives right by my street, and I figure he's taking Maria home first, but then he pulls over right next to the new Kwik Spot and shuts off the car. Then he clears his throat. I look over and see he's leaning over and giving me and Maria a very serious look, like he's mad. "So, you two talked him into this basketball business?"

"Mostly Simon," says Maria. "We didn't think he'd get in trouble."

Then Uncle Jamaal stops frowning and breaks into a huge laugh. Sometimes he plays too much. "Well," he says, "I guess I got you two to thank, then. I've been trying to talk this boy into getting off his butt all winter."

"You should be captain," I say to C.J.

His face kinda falls. "Me? Nah. I'm just happy to play. I'm not the boss of people."

"Don't know till you try," says Uncle Jamaal. "I never wanted to be nobody's boss 'cept my own, but there ain't no reason you couldn't be captain. Knock some respect into that Bobby kid."

C.J. turns to me. "You should do it."

"No one's voting for the air-ball guy as captain," I say.

"Whatever. Everyone'll probably pick Janay cuz she's the coach's kid."

"Maybe, but you should at least try!" I say. Then I turn to Uncle Jamaal. "He is really good."

"Don't you think I know that? He'd probably make the high school team in a few years if he just applied hisself. But I can't have a truck full of hungry Panthers." He nudges his head toward the door to the store. "One snack each."

He must *really* be glad C.J. is playing. He doesn't give out money like that much, and he's the kind of guy who always makes sure people turn out the lights, cuz he ain't paying for rooms to be bright when nobody's in them. But they live in a house all by themselves, so I don't think they're broke or anything.

Even from outside, the Kwik Spot sure looks slick. Just like the Kwik Spots on the North Side and out in the suburbs.

"You see that?" asks C.J. "They sure don't have a glowing sign like that at Wheeler's."

"Why would he need one?" I ask. "Everyone in Creighton Park knows right where he is."

"Just wait till you see inside."

He isn't kidding. On the inside, the Kwik Spot

just shines. Maybe it's cuz it's so gloomy outside, but going into the door is almost like stepping into a movie. It's brighter, the floors are all shiny, and the row of snacks seems like it goes on forever! And he wasn't kidding about the prices, either. The candy bars are a bit cheaper. Even with the coins I scraped out of my pockets, I'll be able to get some Fun Dip. C.J.'s dad is right. This place is like heaven! They got a rack of comic books, too, and a whole section of those "As Seen on TV" gadgets. I feel like I'm in some fancy neighborhood when I'm shopping here. Whole bunch of stuff that Wheeler's wouldn't even have room for.

I THINK I WAS WRONG ABOUT KWIK SPOT!
THEY GOT GADGETS, AND GIZMOS, AND
TOYS, AND TICK-TOCKS.

THE PRICES ARE CHEAPER, THE AISLES ARE
MUCH WIDER.
THE FLOORS ARE SO CLEAN, THE LIGHTS ARE
JUST BRIGHTER.
I FEEL LIKE A KING AS I WALK THROUGH
THE STORE.

"GIMME THIS, GIMME THAT...I WANT ALL THIS
AND MORE!"
AND I BET, IF YOU WANT IT, THEY HAVE IT!
ALL THE BRAND-NEW SNACKS AND THE
CLASSICS!
GON' BE DOPE HAVING THIS STORE AROUND
IN THE HOOD.
YEAH, WHEELER'S IS COOL, BUT KWIK SPOT
IS GOOD!

Uncle Jamaal strolls through the place like a he's a star or something, grinning and chewing on a toothpick.

But Maria seems weird. She's probably thinking about all the stuff her sister was saying about it. As we drive away, she just stares along the road at all the stores and looks like she's reading every sign in every window, like she actually cares about ads for car parts, payday loans, or anything else they have on Locust Street while she nibbles on the Peeps she got.

WEDNESDAY

CHAPTER 9

AIIIRRR BALL.

Airrrr ball.

I can't get those words outta my head. After Uncle Jamaal dropped me off, I heard 'em ringing in my ears while I was eating my dinner and then when I was brushing my teeth. Heard 'em again all this morning while I was eating my cereal. Even my footsteps on the walk to school got the same rhythm.

Aiiiiir.

Ball.

Aiiirrr.

Ball.

I try to shake it off. But it ain't goin' nowhere.

☆ ☆ ☆

When I hand Mr. James my math homework, he says, "Good practice last night, Simon."

"What are you talking about?" I ask. "Didn't you see that air ball?"

"Guess I missed it when I was getting the pretzels, but so what if you airballed? If you were perfect already, we wouldn't have practice."

"Nobody else had one the whole practice."

"Everyone shoots an air ball now and then. Here, come around the desk. Look at this."

I go around and he turns on his computer screen, goes to YouTube, and starts typing in stuff like *NBA* and *air ball.*

Up come all these videos: LeBron airballing. Kevin Durant airballing. Everybody.

"See?" he says. "Happens to everyone except the people who don't play."

It does make me feel a bit better, especially when he finds one of Grayson Allen airballing. I almost even want to join in on shouting "Air ball" and see if I sing just right, but I know Mr. James doesn't like that kind of disrespect, even if it is a kind of magic.

"You gonna put yourself up for captain?" he asks.

"I think it oughta be C.J.," I say. "I been trying to convince him."

Mr. James nods. "I like that. Most kids would want to be captain just for the sake of being captain."

"But you've seen C.J. play," I say. "I really think it should be him."

"You're supporting your friend. That's very mature of you."

Mature. I like the sound of that.

Take that, Aaron. Who's a little kid now?

C.J. got new shoes! They ain't Jordans or anything, but they look so shiny that if you ever saw them, you would even say they glowed.

"With those kicks, you have to be captain," I tell him at lunch. "If you don't do it, Bobby or Victor G.

might get it. Can't count on everyone else to vote for Janay, and anyway, you really want her to do it?"

He shakes his head. "Look at me. I'm a mess. I gotta sit in the back row in class. I had to get some special deal to get extra time on the tests. You really think I got it in me to be a captain?"

"What's having extra time on tests got to do with being the captain? When you talk, people listen. You always know what to say to people."

"What's a captain even do?" Maria asks. "It's a basketball team, not a pirate ship. It's not like the captain has to sail the team, right?"

"A captain is like the unofficial boss of the team," I say. "Keeps things positive. Sets an example. Shakes hands with the other captain before and after the game. Interviews before and after the game."

"Ain't nobody gonna interview us after a rec league game!" he says. "This ain't pro ball."

"So it's an easy job!" I say. "Besides, everyone watching knew you were the best player. Even Bobby and Victor know. They won't admit it, but they know."

"Still sounds like more work," he says. "People don't vote for me for stuff. Everybody just thinks I'm weird."

"I don't!" says Maria.

He glares. "What? You think I'm basic? I take that as an insult!"

"There ain't nothing basic about how your feet smell. That's *extra.* I just mean, some people don't know you like we do. Just cuz you don't participate in class much or organize all the games or turn into a superhero at night doesn't mean you can't be the leader."

"It's like you *do* be a superhero, though," I say. "Like, most of the time you're just C.J., doodling your way through cartoon marathons. But once they have the tip-off, you turn into a star."

He bites a chicken nugget and chews for a long time. "I'll think about it," he says.

But we all know what that means, cuz we all use it too. When you say "I'll think about it," that's a nice way of getting people to stop bugging you about something you ain't gonna do.

CHAPTER 10

BEFORE PRACTICE THAT NIGHT, COACH Thomas gives me a couple of pointers on dribbling. She says I shouldn't look down at the ball so much. My brain and my hand know where the ball's going and where it's coming back to, no need to get my eyes involved. Who woulda thought a hand knew anything? It ain't like they got some tiny brain in my pinky. But it's all connected to your main brain, I guess.

I try it out and it works! The less I look, the better I dribble. She also shows me how to keep my hand low, so the ball doesn't have as far to move. I hit my foot a lot less.

For most of the practice, we all work on our positions; some of the kids—especially the ones who are probably here cuz their parents wanted them to be someone else's problem for a while—haven't ever played anything but street ball or games of Twenty-One or Thirty-Two, so they aren't totally sure what their positions even do.

As the point guard, my job is to start out with the ball and try to figure out where to put it. Do I pass it to C.J. or Bobby? Whoever's open, really. That's most of it, but Mr. James says there's a lot more to it. A lot of brain stuff we'll get to later. Today, we're just focused on the fundamentals. Bustin' our fundaments.

Real talk. When I think about being point guard, it kinda scares me. You know who else was a point guard? Magic Johnson. It feels like a big responsibility. I don't mind doing stuff, but when people *expect* me to do stuff, it turns into this whole other thing.

And the fact that we still kinda stink don't help me none. Coach Thomas runs us on drills, and we mostly mess up. The ball gets thrown into the bleachers. People miss passes. C.J. is still doing great, and Bobby and Victor are still making a lot of shots, but when we try to do a full play, it's a mess every time. Chaos.

Plus, every time I go to shoot, I still hear that sound in my head. "Aiiirrrr ball. Airrrrr ball."

Mr. James tries to help by yelling out some of his quotes, but I think he needs some new ones. It's all stuff we've heard before.

When practice is winding down, Coach Thomas gathers us all together.

"All right," she says. "We need to decide who's the captain."

"I call it!" says Janay.

"That ain't how it works. Before we take up nominations and a vote, let's talk about what a captain does for a basketball team. Who can say what a captain does?"

"Interviews!" shouts Bobby.

"Sure, if that comes up, interviews," says Coach. "But what's something that the captain of the Panthers will definitely have to do?"

"Set an example," I say.

"That's right. What else?"

Louis says something about how the captain is like the middleman for the team with the coach. Stuff like that. And once we all know what the captain has to do, they take up nominations.

"I nominate C.J.," I say. "Everybody knows he the best."

"C.J., you accept the nomination?" asks Coach.

He shrugs and says, "I guess." But he's looking up at the ceiling. I can tell he wishes he had something to doodle on right about then.

"I nominate myself!" says Janay.

"And I nominate Bobby!" says Victor. "He's just as good as C.J., and taller, too."

I gotta admit that's gonna be tough to beat. I mean, by now we all know that taller don't always mean better, but I know that people are pretty impressed by height. *I* should know.

A couple of the other kids nominate themselves, too, since Janay did, but Coach says the rule is you can't vote for yourself. So when we raise our hands to vote, Bobby gets one, Janay gets one, and C.J. gets all the rest!

"Way to go, Captain," I say.

He looks nervous. Or maybe he just looks like he always do.

Uncle Jamaal sure is happy, though. He takes us all to Kwik Spot again. I worked up a pretty good thirst playing, so I head for the drinks. Only I don't see my Duck Island Concord Grape anywhere! Just Crush, Welch's, and all those other big ones, which aren't the same.

When a guy in a blue vest walks by, he asks if he can help me with anything.

"You got any Duck Island Concord Grape?" I ask.

"Oh, I love that stuff!" he says. "But nah, we never have that. It's a local brand."

"You know what's NOT a local brand?" asks C.J. "Flamin' Hot Cheetos!"

He's got a whole handful of them.

I bet if he knew there were Flamin' Hots in it for him, he wouldn't've been so nervous about being captain!

CHAPTER 11

I GO TO C.J.'S PLACE AFTER UNCLE JAMAAL drops off Maria. C.J. lives in one of the smaller versions of those houses across the street from Creighton Crest. No tower or nothing like that, and just two floors, not three or four. But his family got the whole place to themselves! The view out his window ain't as good as mine, and he never gets to pet a neighbor's cat who's out roaming the stairwells like I do sometimes, but if he wanted to practice dribbling in his front room, who'd tell him to stop? If I tried dribbling at our place, Mrs. Coleman downstairs would probably go so wild she'd end up on the news. Even if I just try to practice spinning on my finger, like Maria can, I drop it now and then and she starts yelling.

That's not to say that C.J.'s place is fancy, though. Really, it's always kind of a mess. But I think that's how they like it. At my place Moms always makes sure the pictures are lined up on the wall, all the silverware is separated out in the drawer. "A place for everything, and everything in its place," she says. It's not like that here. Pictures are hung up just wherever, there's art projects scattered all over, and blankets and pillows piled up so high that it's like extra furniture. It's great, really. I sorta wish I could dribble a basketball inside, but I *really* wish my parents didn't mind things looking messy.

We sit in the living room and watch some old movie where this comedian plays a genie. Deijah is on the floor coloring in a coloring book. She's in school, but little enough that coloring is pretty much her whole life. Well, coloring and karate. She loves karate. When I see her color I figure she's gonna be like C.J.—always doodling. But I can't see C.J. taking karate.

C.J.'s seen the movie before, so a lot of time he's drawing on a clipboard. When I look over, I see it's not his regular doodles. It's all circles and lines.

"What're you drawing?"

"Playing diagrams," he says. "Different plays we could run on the court."

"That's the coach's job, isn't it?"

"Yeah, but I'm just trying to learn all the basics. If I'm gonna be the captain, I don't want to let nobody down."

"I should learn it, too," I say. "Point guards gotta know that stuff, right?"

He talks me through some of the moves. Like, one where I pass to him, one where I pass to Bobby, one where I just take the ball and run with it. I'm starting to see more about what Mr. James meant when he said basketball was a mental game. It's not just about running and shooting. You gotta think fast, know how to put the ball where the other team ain't at.

"What you do," says C.J., "is set the tempo. That's almost more important than being captain. Like, if you're moving fast, the rest of us are moving fast. In a fast tempo, the idea is just to get the ball to the hoop before the defense can get there. Slow tempo, it's more about being tricky and working it past them."

"I probably gotta go slow," I say. "None of us are that fast."

"Other team probably isn't fast, either, though," he says. "I mean, none of us are as fast as NBA guys yet. We just do what we can."

I normally only hear C.J. talking like this when he's talking about Fortnite. I came over when he was playing once, and I ain't doing that again. He might space out a lot, but when he's playing Fortnite, he locks right in. The green line L train could go off the track and right through his window, and if he was playing Fortnite, he'd probably never even notice, long as it didn't hit him.

Uncle Jamaal comes in just about the time the movie is wrapping up—I figured out how it was gonna end about five minutes in—and looks over C.J.'s drawings. He nods and makes a couple of comments.

Deijah, this whole time, has been so focused on

coloring that she didn't even look at the movie. She really is like C.J. Hyper-focusing when she needs to. But now she looks up and says, "You know what you should really do?"

"What's that, Deijah?" asks C.J.

She hops up and says, "When they try to get the ball, you go like THIS!" Then she does a couple of side kicks.

"I think that would be a foul," I say.

"You get five fouls a game, right? So you can do it five times."

Uncle Jamaal shakes his head. "That ain't how it works. Especially in rec league. Plus, you side-kick them, they might come side-kick you right back."

Deijah goes into a whole thing of how she'd handle *that*. If she signs up for the Panthers in a few years, they're gonna be carrying the other team out on stretchers! Her karate skills seem just as sharp as her My Little Pony coloring skills.

HI-YAH!

HUH-HUH, HI-YAH!

DEIJAH GON' BRING THAT FI-YA!

'Bout six o'clock C.J.'s mom, Auntie Sharon, comes home from her job braiding hair in the back of Mr. Ray's. I call home to get permission to stay for dinner. Uncle Jamaal is cooking up homemade pizza, and you don't want to miss Jamaal's homemade pizza. He uses different toppings than you get other places: barbecue chicken, sport peppers, even cactus! I don't know where the heck he even gets a cactus!

Uncle Jamaal can seem kinda weird, just like C.J. But before he started working like he does, he was an artist full-time, and he's still an artist at heart. You can see it in his pizza.

After a couple slices, Auntie Sharon says, "Mr. Ray's getting nervous about that coffee shop."

"It's a coffee shop, Sharon," says Uncle Jamaal.

"No one's gonna go get their hair cut at the coffee shop."

"You know what I mean," says Auntie Sharon. "First they bring in a big coffee shop, and then the rent goes up."

"Business goes up, too. You want that giant bank building to just get torn down?"

"You mean that one bank?" C.J. asks. "The one that looks like something outta *Indiana Jones*?"

Uncle Jamaal nods. "Been sitting empty for years, but they turned it into a big coffee shop. Thinking about adding a museum into it, too."

I know which bank he means. It's as big as my whole apartment building, and it looks like something from ancient Egypt. Another one of those places around Creighton that must have been really fancy when they built it.

"It's more than the coffee shop," says Auntie Sharon. "Two of those houses on the block just sold and the people who are moving in... they're artists."

Uncle Jamaal has a mouthful of pizza, but he spreads his arms out. "What do you think *I* am? You see all the art in this place?"

"I know, I know. But it's just…it's always how it starts. First the artists come in, then the twenty-somethings, then the rich people, and next thing you know there's a Supercuts where Mr. Ray's used to be." She looks down at the pizza, then back up. "Where'd you get the cactus for this?"

"A carnicería down in Little Village. You know, that one where they make tacos in the back? I was working out by there, so I stocked up."

Auntie Sharon relaxes a bit. "That's all right, then."

I guess she doesn't like him going to Kwik Spot much. I think she thinks a lot of the same stuff as Maria's sister about people shopping too much or whatever. Uncle Jamaal never worries about that stuff.

I didn't realize Mr. Ray was getting worried, though. I had almost forgotten that Mr. Wheeler seemed like he was a bit worried when he was talking to Mr. Ray, too.

Seem like everybody in Creighton is low-key worried.

Should I be worried, too?

THURSDAY

CHAPTER 12

TODAY, MR. JAMES HAS FIRED UP THE SMART board, and there's a big, long word—the kind Moms calls a Fifty-Cent Word—up on it.

GENTRIFICATION

I sit down and take off my hoodie. The radiators don't work right all the time, but sometimes they work too good. Today is one of those days. We gotta get all bundled up to get to school, but once we're in there, it's roasting. If you don't peel off a layer, you'll get home medium rare and ready to eat.

Mr. James told us that radiators are supposed to be used with windows *open*. They were invented back when there was a nasty flu going around, and people thought you should keep the windows open to keep from catching it. Only whoever thought of that must not have been from the Chi. No one's gonna open a window during a winter here, even if it feels like an oven inside.

"All right, scholars," he says. "I'm sure you've all been noticing some interesting things happening in our neighborhood, like new shops and the construction barrels going up."

"Kwik Spot!" blurts out Lil Kenny. "It just opened, and I see all kinds of people shopping in there now."

"Like people who wouldn't come to this neighborhood to shop before," adds Victor.

Mr. James nods and points to the board. "Who can sound this word out?"

"*Gen-tri-fi-ca-tion*," says Maria. "My sister says that word a lot."

"I'll bet she does!" says Mr. James. "I should have known it wouldn't take long for one of you-all to know the word. But do you know what it means?"

"Something to do with money."

Mr. James nods. "That's part of it, yes. So, let's stop looking at the whole word, and break it into parts."

Here he goes again with how words are made of old ones.

He draws a line down the middle of the word on the SMART Board.

GENTRI—FICATION

He points at the part on the right. "*Fication*. Where have we seen that before?"

"Like *notification*," says Victor.

"Right!" Mr. James smiles. "You get a notification when you're notified, and you get gentrification when you're . . . gentrified."

Then he just writes one word:

GENTRY

"*Gentry*. Where have we seen this word?"

"*Tree!*" shouts Kenny, even though he probably knows it's wrong.

"Not exactly. Anything else?"

No one says nothing, so he erases the last two letters.

GENT

"Oh!" I say. "Like *gentleman*!"

"Exactly, Mr. Barnes. *Gentleman*. Now, where do we see that word? What's a gentleman?"

"Someone who has to pee," says Kenny.

Mr. James fixes him with a look. "Everyone does that from time to time, don't they?"

"But that's where you see that word now," says Kenny. "Some of our bathroom doors say *Ladies* or *Gentlemen*. Where else you see it?"

He's got a point! You hear people say "ladies

and gentlemen," but even Mr. James can't think of another place where you SEE it.

"Mr. James, I'm a gentleman right now!" says Kenny. "Can I go to the gentlemen's room?"

"One moment," says Mr. James. "But the point is: Yes. *Gentry* is like *gentlemen*. It's from the French word *gentil*, which meant 'noble.' So, a gentleman is like a nobleman. Or at least, back in the old days. Today we see *gentlemen* as a way to say *men* when you want to be all fancy. But in the old days, only rich men were called gentlemen."

Kenny jumps right on that one.

"So, if you went up to the restroom, and it said *Gentlemen*, you had to be rich to go in?"

"I'm talking about back before toilets were invented," says Mr. James. "Before places had public restrooms."

"So, everybody just peed on themselves?" asks Kenny.

"That's a question for another time," says Mr. James. "But the thing is: back in the old days, being a gentleman meant you were rich, and the rich people in town were called the gentry."

But what *did* people do back before they had public restrooms? Like, what if you went out to some big old-timey market or to see knights fighting it out, and you had to go? What did you do?

This is the kind of stuff they *should* be teaching in social studies. Instead we just talk about buildings and stuff.

Mr. James sings a bit of a song about how you can ask the local gentry about something, but we all boo. He's a much better rapper than he is a singer! He does his hand thing to quiet us down, but he knows he asked for it.

"OH EM GEE, y'all. He ain't *that* bad."

"Thanks, Maria. I think."

"Gotchu."

"So, anyway, we're down to two word parts," Mr. James says. "*Gentry* and *fication*. So what do you think the whole word means?"

"Rich-guy-ification!" I call out. "Can I get some of that right now?"

He smiles. "You sure you want it, Mr. Barnes?"

"One hundred percent." If I was rich, I could get the Panthers new basketballs and uniforms.

Then maybe we would play better. "Yeah, I want to be rich-guy-ified!"

"So that is what we'll be talking about in social studies," he says. "A lot of neighborhoods get gentrified. Rich people move in. And sometimes there's good things. You might get a cool new coffee shop. They might finally tear down the buildings that are empty and just waiting to catch fire. But as things get fancier, rents go up. Prices go up. And the old businesses, even the good ones, start to close, and the people who lived in the apartments might not be able to afford them anymore."

"But don't we want our neighborhood to get nicer?" asks Bobby.

"Of course," says Mr. James. "And that's why we have social studies. Because it's complicated. We all want our neighborhoods to be nicer, but we don't want to get rich-guy-ified right out of them."

CHAPTER 13

THE REST OF THE DAY, I KEEP THINKING about what Mr. James talked about. But once I get to the rec center, I forget all about it because there are two people I don't recognize standing on the sidelines, and they're both holding clipboards.

That's weird.

"Who are they?" I ask C.J. "They look important."

C.J. shrugs. "Who knows?"

I can't worry too much about it because Coach Thomas blows her whistle. "All right, Panthers. Today we're going to start with a two-line lay-up drill."

First, Coach lines us up on opposite sidelines. Then she passes the ball to Janay, who dribbles up to the basket and shoots. The ball bounces off the rim, so the rebound goes to Victor. He dribbles and passes to the next person in line on the opposite side, which is me. When I go for the layup, the ball spins around on the rim before falling off the side, right into C.J.'s waiting hands. And on and on until we all get a turn to dribble, pass, and shoot on each side.

Coach runs us through a few more drills: three-man weave, a three-on-two fast-break transition drill, and a lot of passing drills.

After we're good and warmed up, Coach gathers us around. "Now we're going to do an exercise called King of the Court." She nods to me and Victor. "You two, head to the three-point line.

"Now, Simon, you need to make a shot, but the trick is that you only get up to three dribbles to do it. Victor, you need to do everything to block Simon from making that basket."

Victor laughs. "Ain't no way Shorty Simon can make a shot."

Mr. James blows his whistle. "Not cool, Victor."

"That's right," Coach Thomas adds. "There's nothing wrong with clowning on each other on the court, but I draw the line at being mean." She looks around at us all, then goes back to telling us the rules. "You make that basket, you get a point and the defender gets switched out for another defender. You don't make the shot, you move off the court and the defender takes a turn. First person to score five points is the King of the Court. Got it?"

I got it, but I don't know if I *got* it, feel me? That basket is looking farther away than ever. What if I choke again? If I can't even make a free throw, how am I supposed do this?

And those two strange people are watching me like a hawk.

"Bawk-bok!" Victor says it low enough that the coaches can't hear, but I can hear. And you know what? It makes me so mad I forget to dribble. I just shoot the ball. And it goes in! What the heck? I make these, but not free throws?

"One point for Simon," Coach says. "Victor, you're off. Louis, you're up."

Victor makes a face at me, but he joins the others on the sideline.

I shoot again, but my luck doesn't hold out. The ball don't come close to the hoop, but nobody says "Air ball" this time. I guess because everybody knows making a three-pointer is way harder than making a free throw.

For most people anyway.

Louis makes it look simple, but eventually he gets taken down by Janay after three baskets. Most of the team ain't taking it as serious, so once Janay is defeated, people start dropping like flies. But since everybody needs a chance to shoot and a chance to defend, it takes up almost the whole rest of practice. But then it's C.J.'s turn. He gets the same look on his face like when he's doodling or playing Fortnite.

And he makes FOUR shots in a row! By now, we're making so much noise Mr. James has to blow his whistle again. But the noise don't stop C.J. *Swish!* He makes that fifth basket, easy.

We lose our minds. Everybody is dapping C.J. up, and I gotta be honest, this is lit! I'm proud he is the captain and I'm glad he is my best friend.

Coach blows her whistle to get us to settle down. "Nice work. All of you. But now it's time to let a *real* player play." She takes off her whistle, grabs the ball, and points to Victor. "Try and stop me."

Coach scores not one, two, or three baskets. She scores eight three-pointers in a row, showing *everybody* up. *Swish, swish, swish!* She makes it look as easy as anything. We can't believe it!

"And that's how you become Queen of the Court!" she yells. Then she ruffles Janay's hair. "Let's eat some pretzels!"

CHAPTER 14

AFTER I GET HOME FROM PRACTICE, ME, Dad, Markus, and DeShawn all go to Mr. Ray's for fresh cuts. We usually go on Saturday, but I need the freshest cut possible. Tomorrow is game day!

Aaron's already there sweeping up, so Markus and DeShawn spend the whole time we're waiting teasing him.

"You missed a spot!" shouts Markus.

"Y'all gonna get this broomstick up your nose if you don't watch y'all's mouth," he snaps back.

Everybody in the place laughs.

If Mr. Ray is nervous about the new coffee shop, or anything else, he doesn't show it.

"All right, Rhymin' Simon," he says. "Hop up."

"Everybody gotta make room, tell my brother to watch the broom!"

People laugh a bit. Sometimes I get nervous rapping at the open mic or in front of people, but dropping a rhyme or two at Mr. Ray's? It's different.

"Hi, Mr. Ray," I say.

Mr. Ray is the one person you don't clown on.

Some of the older guys do, but I think you have to be at least fifty before you do anything that even *looks* like disrespecting the barber. Even then, you're taking a pretty big risk if you disrespect the guy who's about to give you a haircut. He might get his revenge by making you look like a fool!

"First Panthers game of the season!" he says as I sit down. "You ready to make Creighton Park proud?"

"We got a decent team," I say. "You just gotta remember, basketball is a mental game, not just a tall people game."

Somebody says something about Muggsy Bogues, and then I say something back about Spud Webb. Pretty soon the whole barbershop is talking. That's the thing about Mr. Ray's: You might not be able to diss Mr. Ray, even joking, but everybody here is one of the grown-ups.

When things are quieter, I ask him what he thinks about the coffee shop going in.

"Guess it's better than an empty building," he says. "But I got all the coffee I need in the pot in the back."

"C.J.'s dad says no one's gonna get their hair cut at a coffee shop," I say.

"Sure hope that's right!" Mr. Ray laughs. "Now, Aaron, get up over here and sweep up your brother's hair! You helping this boy with his basketball?"

"Soon as I can find some time," says Aaron. "Been pretty busy."

"Now that ain't no excuse!" says Mr. Ray. "The Panthers are a Creighton tradition, and it's your responsibility to make sure you pass on every bit of knowledge you got."

"That ain't much!" shouts Markus.

"Hey!" says Aaron. "Scoring leader!"

"Exactly," says Mr. Ray. "Look. Sunday, you take off an hour early and get this boy on the court. I'll let you be on the clock. Call it my donation to the Panthers."

"Yes, Mr. Ray."

Now Aaron seems excited—he rubs my shoulder. And no wonder! Now he's gonna get paid an hour's work to play basketball!

In a way, that makes him a professional basketball player.

I bet I never hear the end of that.

I just wish we could go today. But it's already dark out.

When my cut is finished, Mr. Ray pats me on the back and says, "Do Creighton Park proud, Rhymin' Simon. We need all the help we can get!"

FRIDAY

CHAPTER 15

THE BLUE JERSEYS WE'RE WEARING AREN'T brand-new or anything, but when I put mine on and walk into the rec center, it feels like I'm putting on armor. I never had a uniform before, even one that was passed down through generations of Creighton Park Panthers.

The team is gathering around in one corner, where Mr. James is passing out water bottles while Coach Thomas runs a few drills with Janay and C.J.

"You're getting this stuff," Coach says. "Y'all have come a long way!"

"We got a long way to go!" says Janay.

"It's all right. We'll get there. I'm proud of where you all are already."

On the other side of the court, the Lawndale Tornadoes are warming up. I've been telling myself that the other teams are gonna be just as rough around the edges as us, but they look like they've been playing a lot longer than we have.

A few minutes before tip-off time, we all gather around in a huddle, and I notice something: Bobby and Louis ain't here! I shoulda known since it was quiet. Not one person has ripped me about having a new haircut, which Bobby would normally do no matter how smooth I looked.

C.J. looks at Victor G. "Where's Bobby and his cousin?"

"I ain't heard from him," he says. "They'll be here."

But a couple more minutes go by and now it's time for tip-off. Ain't no sign of either of them!

"I guess we'll have to play without them," says Mr. James.

"We're dead meat without them," says Janay. "They're the best players we got!"

"Ahem!" I say. "Best except for C.J. You just being dramatic."

"Okay, fine, C.J.'s the best. But without them, we don't have a chance! I say we forfeit and just go have snacks now."

I hate to say it, but she's right. Bobby isn't my favorite person, and it's nice not to get insulted all the time, but we need him out there on the court. He's good. So is Louis. Without them we're in big trouble.

"Well, we got enough players, so the show must go on," says Coach Thomas. Mr. James opens his mouth, like he's about to say the thing about giving 110 percent, but Coach says, "Would our team captain like to say a few words to get us all pumped up?"

C.J. isn't staring at the ceiling or looking like he wishes he could do some doodling right about now. He is zeroed right in on us.

"Okay, Panthers," he says. "We've all been working hard. Just as hard as the Tornadoes, I bet. We might be missing a couple of people, but they don't know that. Creighton on three. One, two, three!"

We all shout "Creighton!" and for just a minute I feel like we got this. Nothing can stop us!

But that feeling only lasts till about twenty seconds after tip-off.

The Tornadoes seem like they got the right name—they blow right through us. They run circles around us. It's a wonder we don't get blown straight into Lake Michigan or whatever. Without Bobby and Louis, we're hopeless.

I get the ball to C.J. now and then, but setting tempo? I'm hopeless. Passing? All over the place. Dribbling? All over my toes. I get called for traveling twice. Just about every point we score is a free throw, and all twelve of them are by C.J.

IT'S OUR FIRST GAME AND WE'RE GETTING
BEAT BAD.
EVERYTHING IS GOING WRONG, AND IT'S JUST
SO SAD.
PLUS WE'RE DOWN A COUPLE PLAYERS, SO WE
FEEL SO WEAK.
COULDA USED AN EXTRA PRACTICE, OR FIVE
MORE, AT LEAST!

WE STINK! WE REEK! THE WHOLE TEAM SMELLS
ANYONE WHO'S WATCHING US COULD
DEFINITELY TELL.
WE NOT PLAYING AS A TEAM, WE DON'T LOOK
LIKE WE GEL.
THIS AIN'T PANTHERS BASKETBALL, IT'S NOT
GOING WELL.

THE SCORE...WELL...IT'S 43 TO 12!
WE GETTING BLOWN OUT...THIS IS AN
EPIC FAIL.
NO ONE WOULD BE PROUD, NOT WHEELER,
NOT SUNNY,
NOT MARKUS OR DESHAWN, THOUGH, THEY'D
PROBABLY THINK IT'S FUNNY

HOW AIR BALL BARNES AND HIS TEAMMATES
ARE WACK!
NOTHING COACH T. SAYS COULD HELP BRING US
BACK!
NOT EVEN LEBRON JAMES COULD HELP US WIN
THIS GAME.
IT'S A BIG L FOR CREIGHTON, AND I'M NOT
TALKIN' 'BOUT NO TRAIN!

There's no partying or cheering when the game ends. I'm just glad it's over after we shake hands with the Tornadoes and say, "Good game." I kinda appreciate that they say it, cuz they gotta know we did *not* play a good game.

And as soon as we're done, I just walk over to the wall and sit down. This is humiliating. Being as short as I am doesn't help, but all that stuff about how it's a mental game? That didn't help me, either. I was even giving 110 percent! No quote's gonna get me out of this.

About the only good thing is that there weren't many people here to see it. Maybe it's just one of those things like how when you're really little you think every adult is a giant, but I feel like when I went to my brothers' Panthers games, the bleachers always had a lot of people in them. Today, it looks like just parents, maybe a couple of brothers and sisters. But no one from Creighton Park came. And it's not *that* cold out.

Maybe I should just quit. Me being here ain't helping them any. Even the kids who normally don't seem like they even want to be there were playing better than me once they got in the game. Maybe the best thing I could do for Creighton would be just to bounce.

C.J. comes walking over.

"Come on," he says. "Mr. James is gonna take us all out to Mr. Wheeler's, see if he's got any hot pickles in."

"What are we celebrating?" I ask. "We just got ground into glue. Which might as well be what's on my shoes. I'ma quit."

"What are you talking about?" he asks. "We need you out there!"

"Didn't you see me? I didn't score one point. I traveled. I dribbled on my feet, even after Coach taught me how not to!"

"It's just one game, man. Stop feeling sorry for yourself. Didn't you say Aaron was taking you out to practice on Sunday?"

"Yeah."

"Then at least see what you can learn first. And anyway, it's not like this team was good last year. Ain't had a winning season in years. What's one more?"

The way he's smiling helps. I don't feel better, exactly, but at least I don't feel like I totally let him down. By the end of the game I felt like he'd probably never smile again and it was all my fault. I still feel like I'm probably holding him back stinking up the court like that, but he's right: It ain't like the Panthers were all that good to start with.

"Come on," Mr. James calls. "We're all walking over to Wheeler's."

We all gather up, put on our coats, and all of us, plus our parents, walk down the street. Moms and Dad pat me on the back and tell me not to worry—just keep listening to Coach, and practice with Aaron, and I'll get better. I'm kinda glad they don't seem like I let them down. Markus and DeShawn don't say nothing. Partly cuz it's not like the Panthers won much when they were on the team, and probably partly because clowning on me after I got beat that hard would just be too mean.

But when I think about it, I know they'd clown me to death if I quit.

Speaking of clowning, you know who seems real quiet? Victor. As we walk, he isn't saying anything.

"What happened to Bobby?" I ask.

"I still ain't heard from him," he says. "Maybe... maybe he just didn't want to play with a bunch of losers."

Guess I couldn't blame him. But without Bobby around, Victor seems kinda harmless. Trouble is, he's harmless on the court, too!

When we get to the store, something's wrong: Wheeler's isn't open!

"That's weird," says Mr. James.

A sign on the window says CLOSED AT 6PM TODAY. SORRY FOR THE INCONVENIENCE.

Closed on a Friday night? He must be sick or something. Gotta be.

"Why don't we just go to Kwik Spot over on Locust?" asks C.J.

"Come on back to my truck," says Uncle Jamaal. "I can fit two besides C.J. I know they're open!"

Mr. James sighs out loud. "I'm afraid that might be why Wheeler's is closed early."

Dad drives me over to Kwik Spot, and I get a different kind of grape pop.

But it's not the same. Not nearly as good. Must be made with just regular grapes, not Concord. In fact, there's probably never been anything close to a grape in it. They could at least use *good* artificial grapes.

And somehow, I feel like even if it was Duck Island Concord, coming from Kwik Spot after a game like that, it'd still leave a bad taste in my mouth.

SUNDAY

CHAPTER 16

I'M STILL FEELING DOWN WHEN I WAKE UP Sunday morning, but I drag myself out of bed anyway. It's the Community Outreach Open Mic, and I need to be there to set it up.

I can't let Creighton Park down like I did Friday night.

The monthly Creighton Park Community Outreach Open Mic is where anybody that wants to can come speak their mind about what's going on in Creighton, read a poem, sing a song. Just whatever, as long as it's respectful. Something to let their voices be heard without just standing around on a street corner.

Also: No selling stuff. Had a couple come in and try to push some get-rich-quick schemes that would prolly make everybody broke.

Only when I get to the community center, it's looking like it's gonna be pretty slow. Not many people are signing up, and most of the people hanging around are the people who are here all the time. Like Sunny. When it's warm, he's always out in the neighborhood, sweeping up, just to do it. He doesn't shovel snow much anymore, though. It's starting to get too hard on his back.

"Rhymin' Simon!" he says. "You got a rap about all this cold?"

He laughs. And then I feel weird, cuz every other open mic we've had I've worked on a rap to share. This time, I been so worked up about the Panthers that I ain't got one ready! I start to panic a bit, but Sunny has a good idea. I'll rap something about the winter. *"Cold cold, go away, come again no other day,"* I say.

For Sunny's turn at the mic, he sings a song. He always sings. Old blues songs and stuff like that.

Says it's comforting to him, like a nice warm bowl of macaroni and cheese. He's always happy when I see him, but never happier than when he gets to sing.

Since no one else is up on the list, Maria practices a speech she's working on for the debate team into the mic, then I go up and do my thing.

IT'S SUPER-DUPER COLD RIGHT OUTSIDE
THOSE DOORS
AND THE GROUND IS SLIPPERY, LIKE MOPPIN'
A FLOOR.

THERE'S ICE EVERYWHERE, SO DON'T TRIP
AND FALL!
IT KINDA REMINDS ME OF PANTHERS BASKETBALL.

WE WERE COLD AS ICE, WITH EVERY SINGLE
SHOT.
NO POSSIBLE WAY THAT WE COULD GET HOT.
IN THE VERY FIRST GAME, JUST STARTIN'
THE SEASON,

IT FELT LIKE OUR HANDS AND FINGERS WERE
FREEZIN'!

THE BALL WAS FLYIN' EVERYWHERE, LIKE IT WAS
MADE OF SNOW.
EVERYWHERE, OF COURSE, EXCEPT WHERE IT
WAS 'SPOSE TO GO!
THE TORNADOES WERE HOT LIKE A BIG BOWL
OF SOUP,
BUT US? WE COULD BARELY GET THE BALL
NEAR THE HOOP!

I KNOW WE'RE BETTER THAN THAT, AT LEAST I
HOPE WE ARE!
MY FRIEND C.J., HE COULD REALLY BE A STAR!
THE REST OF US NEED WORK, OR AN NBA
MENTOR
OR ELSE WE'LL STAY COLD LIKE A CHI-TOWN
WINTER!

Man, that's what I'm talking about. Everyone seems to dig it. The response I get for rapping sure is different than what I get for basketball playing.

Aaron shows up when we're putting everything away. "You ready to practice?"

"Go," Maria says. "Me and Sunny can handle the rest."

Aaron dribbles down the sidewalk as we walk along. "What kind of problems did you have in the game?"

"Name a problem, I had it!" I say. "I traveled. When I didn't travel, I dribbled off my feet. I didn't make a shot. Everybody just walked all over me."

"Sounds about right. I shoulda taught you some moves a long time ago."

This is nice in a way I can't really even explain. Like, I don't remember the last time Aaron and I just talked like this. Or, anyway, the last time he talked to me like he *wanted* to talk to me. For the longest time, it's felt like he thought he was a grown-up now and I was just some baby.

"You like working at Mr. Ray's?" I ask.

"It's work. It's all right. Think I'd rather be the barber than the sweeper, though."

"You wanna be a barber?"

He laughs. "More than I wanna be sweeping floors. People clown on Mr. Ray, but you know they like him. They're a lot harder on the teenager with a broom. That's all."

"Moms and Dad might flip if you said you didn't want to be a lawyer or something."

He shrugs. "I wanna go to college, see what's out there. You shouldn't go around deciding your whole life before you're grown. But look. You know Mr. Ray's father and grandfather were barbers?"

"Uh-huh."

"And further back. He says his great-great-great-something-grandpa was a guy named Lewis Isbell, and he had a barbershop in Chicago back before the Loop was even called the Loop. Cut hair for Abraham Lincoln when he was in town. Shaved him, too, back before he grew a beard, and then he used being a barber to listen in on people who were thinking of messing with the Union during the Civil War. Helped more than a thousand people escape on the Underground Railroad. Think about that. A thousand!"

"For real?"

"Mr. Ray says so. Course, I don't know if it's all true, but look now. Mr. Ray is the eyes and ears of

Creighton Park. He ain't the alderman or the mayor or whatever, but he's got all the power they do around here, and nobody hate him like they hate on the alderman. Don't seem so bad."

Aldermen are like mayors of neighborhoods. Dad and Moms call ours up every now and then if there's a pothole or something, and the alderman is supposed to take care of it. Sometimes they actually do it. But I ain't never heard nobody talk about how great the alderman was, so maybe Aaron's got a point. There's nobody that don't like Mr. Ray.

Plus, Mr. Ray let Aaron spend an hour *on the clock* just to play basketball with me. You gotta respect a guy like that. Bet the people at the Kwik Spot never get to do that.

"I don't think I want to be a barber," says Aaron. "And I sure ain't trying to sweep up floors for life. But what he's got—that's important. I think we should find ways to make other places have that same feel. Something with technology. Only by the time I'm done with school, all the tech's gonna be way different, probably. So I gotta wait and figure it out later."

I bet Aaron could figure it out now. Sometimes I feel like he's about twice as smart as DeShawn and Markus put together. But maybe it's just cuz he's older, and maybe it's just cuz he snores less than they do.

We get to the court, and Aaron shoots a few baskets, then I shoot a few to warm up. I even make one! Since it's so cold out, no one else is here to get in the way. Most times on a Sunday afternoon, the court'd be full of high school guys playing five-on-five.

"So, you're the point guard, right?" he says.

"Uh-huh. If you can call anything I do a position."

He dribbles a bit, going behind his back. Showing off.

"Now, to start with, you know 'bout guys like Isaiah Thomas, right? Nate Robinson."

"If anything I'm getting tired of hearing about them," I say. "Spud Webb could still dunk. I couldn't dunk even if I started off jumping from a trampoline!"

"Okay. But let's think about it. How could they take being short and make it a strength?"

"If I knew that, I wouldn't need help!"

He laughs a bit, then passes me the ball. "Here. Dribble it a bit."

I dribble, being realllllllllly careful not to hit my shoes. Just slowly, carefully, like Coach Thomas was showing me. I can do it fine when I'm not playing a game, I guess!

"All right," he says. "Now look." He kneels down and holds out his hand. "When you dribble, the ball only goes between here—the ground—and here. That makes it really hard for a tall guy to reach in and steal from you." He stands back up and shows how he'd have to bend over and be really fast to reach in and get it from me. I never thought about it like that! But it's true.

Then he takes the ball and dribbles. "Now, when a tall guy's dribbling, the ball has a longer way to go. And you're already down there, so you got about the whole time the ball is away from his hand to reach in and get it. Try."

We practice a bit, and he lets me try to steal from him and go for the hoop. He keeps it away from me at first, but then I kinda learn his moves, and reach in and get the ball. Once I do, I can run around him so fast he doesn't have time to bend down!

"That's it!" he says. "That's my man! Panthers!"

We work at it. At first it feels like he's letting me steal, and probably he is. But then he starts getting tougher, and I can tell he's doing his best. But I'm still stealing! And after one time, I even get the ball, run to the basket, and shoot it right in. Nothing but net. If I'd played like this Friday...well, we still would've lost, but I wouldn't have been so down afterwards.

"Okay," he says. "One more thing. We gotta work on your trash-talking. Watch."

He has me dribble while he tries to steal. At first it's hopeless, then he starts calling me shorty and I get distracted, and he almost gets it.

"Mr. James don't want us doing all that trash talk," I say.

"Ah! Mr. James! Your rapping teacher! Where'd he learn to be a teacher? The Disney Channel?"

He smacks the ball out of my hands when he says that.

"That wasn't nice!" I say.

"I didn't mean it. It's just game talk. But you know what the point of trash talk is, don't you?"

"What?"

"To distract the other guy. Just worked. Had you thinking about me dissing your teacher, and while you were thinking that, I got the ball."

I nod. It did work.

"It don't gotta be trash, even," he says. "If he's

thinking about what you're saying, no matter what it is, then his head ain't in the game. And that's where you got a skill none of the other guys have."

"Yeah?"

"Rhymin'."

I never thought of that!

He's right. People always call it trash talk, but it don't gotta be disrespectful. I mean, I could probably tell a knock-knock joke on the court and it'd work just as good as saying some trash.

So he has me try it. I start dribbling, he starts trying to block me, and I just start trying to rhyme.

"Basketball, basketball, round and orange..."

Then I freeze up. Nothing rhymes with *orange*!

When I'm a famous rapper I'ma make sure I never play a concert anywhere that's also a basketball arena, like United Center. Something about being on a court just makes the Notorious D.O.G. choke!

"It's all right," Aaron says. "You don't have to be freestyling in the game. Think of a bunch of rhymes ahead of time. Being prepared ain't cheating."

"Failing to prepare is preparing to fail," I say. "That's one of Mr. James's favorite quotes."

"Practice 'em so you don't even have to think about it," says Aaron. "Then *they* get stuck thinking, and you're just thinking of the game!"

I start to think of a few, and pretty soon I'm trying it out. It almost works on Aaron, and if it almost works on Aaron, it'll definitely work against another rec league team.

I feel like my dribbling's getting better. Just the confidence boost I needed. Aaron's right! Everybody's gotta find their own style in basketball, and now I'm finding mine.

Rhymes? From Notorious D.O.G.? They ain't gonna know what hit 'em!

We shoot a few more and I'm feeling a lot better.

I mean, I feel better about basketball, but mostly I feel better about Aaron. For once, he didn't treat me like a baby! I'm like a whole high schooler up in here.

Look out, rec league. Creighton is coming at you!

MONDAY

CHAPTER 17

ON THE WALK TO SCHOOL, MARIA SAYS SHE knows what's up with Bobby and Louis. I don't know how, but Maria always knows everything about everybody. Even Mr. Ray probably got nothing on her! "Who told you all this stuff?"

"Don't worry about it, lil homie. Can't just be givin' up all my info!"

"That's cold, Maria."

"Nah, this weather is what's cold."

Good one.

"They went to go play for the Wildcats. Garfield Park," she says. "They got that new field house, with new courts and new basketballs. Scottie Pippen was there when they opened it, even."

"But they're from Creighton!"

Maria shrugs. "Seems like they wanted to go pro, I guess. The Wildcats won the most games out of anyone the last two seasons."

"Well, no wonder, if they can steal all the good players off the other teams!"

What are those two thinking? This is rec league, not pro. And even then, I remember back in first grade when I found out most of the Chicago Bulls ain't even from Chicago. I get it now. In pro ball, you go where they sign you, but this ain't pro ball. I guess there's no rule saying you can't sign up for any team you want, but we're supposed to be representing our neighborhood!

It all seems more important now, too. As we pass the park, Mr. Wheeler's, and all the stuff that makes Creighton what it is, that makes it feel like it's home, it feels like every bit I do to improve my game is helping the neighborhood. Maybe it's only a tiny little bit, but if I'm gonna be representing, I want to do it the best I can.

But most important, I can't quit. No way.

I'M FROM CREIGHTON PARK, SO CREIGHTON'S
WHERE I'LL PLAY.
NO MATTER WHO SWITCHES UP, I'M ALWAYS
GONNA STAY.
GOTTA REP MY HOOD, IT'S THE BEST IN
CHI-TOWN.
EVEN WHEN OTHERS LEAVE, I WON'T EVER LET
IT DOWN!
THIS PLACE IS HOME, NO PLACE ELSE IS REALER.
WE GOT BOOKER T., MR. RAY'S, AND
MR. WHEELER'S.
THE BEST OUT WEST, WE THE NEIGHBORHOOD
WITH HEART.
THE NOTORIOUS D.O.G., HE LOVES
CREIGHTON PARK!
WOOF WOOF!

But at lunch, C.J. seems bugged. "You think it was their idea to switch? Bobby and Louis?"

"From what I hear, a coach called them up and talked them into it after he saw them at practice. That might be wrong, though."

"Then why didn't he call me?" asks C.J. "I'm playing better than those two!"

"Maybe they knew they couldn't steal the captain," I say.

He shrugs, but I can tell it bugs him.

When we go outside for recess, Bobby is standing by the old bike racks.

"Hey, Barnes!" he says. "I heard you stunk up the court!"

"Yeah?" I say. "I *know* you stinking up the school right now. At least I showed up!"

"Showed up to play for a stinko team with crummy old equipment. Who needs it? I got a good team now."

One thing I notice: Victor ain't hanging around by Bobby today. He's off by himself, looking like he's upset. Why wouldn't he be? His friend is calling him stinko over here. And he ditched him! He ditched his hood *and* his best friend, all just to play for a team where the basketballs still got good grip?

If we got a big new basketball court so people wouldn't quit their teams and go play for some other neighborhood? Would that be bad?

Does this tie in to Mr. Ray being worried, and maybe even to Wheeler's being closed Friday?

Too many questions bouncing around in my head. I'm finna feel like Kenny: Open a door and I'll go running and screaming, just to get it all out.

☆ ☆ ☆

When Bobby goes back to shooting hoops, Victor comes over to us.

"Hey, Captain," he says. "I'm thinking...I'm gonna quit the Panthers."

"You too?" asks C.J. "I just about got Simon talked out of it, and now you?"

"My friend quit on me," he said. "And he didn't even tell me!"

"You mad at him?" I ask.

He doesn't really answer, just kinda makes a face. He don't want to say it, but I can tell he's mad.

"If you quit, y'all barely got enough people to play at all," says Maria. "What people gon' think of

Creighton Park if we can't even keep enough people on the court?"

"Same thing half of them think of us now!" Victor says. "You ever watch the news?"

"Not really."

"Well, they almost never say nothing good about us on there. People are starting to buy up the buildings to tear 'em down, and people think it don't even matter. It's just Creighton. Whole city'd be better off if the whole neighborhood got built over again."

"All the more reason you gotta play!" says C.J. "Bobby and Louis gave up on us, but we gotta show 'em. We gotta show everybody."

"We can't possibly beat their team," says Victor. "Look at us. You saw us. They could put together a team of the oldest, wrinkliest people at the nursing home and they'd still probably beat us."

"Maybe we should ask 'em to," says C.J. "Those old people, they get lonely, you know?"

"For real. Don't knock the old people. My abuela can kick all y'all's butts and you know it," Maria says.

"Come on, Victor," I say. "You want *me* to be the second-best player on the team?"

He looks at me and tilts back his head. "If I'm gone, you ain't second. Janay's way better than you."

"Fine," I say. "But still. We already lost them. What'd they go over there for, anyway?"

"What you think? Better equipment. Better team. Better courts. If my dad would give me a ride over there, I'd be playing there instead, too! But now all Bobby does is mess with me for playing with you bunch of losers. And you see who we play this Friday?"

"Who?" I ask.

"The Wildcats! They'll kick our butt, and then Bobby'll never stop talking about it."

"Don't be such a chicken," says C.J. "Sometimes I go into Fortnite levels knowing I'm not gonna win. Sometimes, you gotta take the hit. You feel like a bigger loser if you don't try."

"Come on, man," I say. "We gotta at least show them Creighton ain't all quitters."

"And you're good," says C.J. "Biggest problem last week is we'd done all our practicing planning on having Bobby and Louis on the team. Without them, it messed up all the plans."

"It messed up the tempo," I add.

"Kinda like that," says C.J. "Yeah. Look, at least come to practice. We're gonna figure out how to play with the team we got, and then we'll all have some pretzels. And if you quit, Mr. James won't never let you hear the end of it, either."

Victor smiles a tiny bit. "They do have good pretzels," he says. "The ones with the big chunks of salt."

"Gotta start somewhere," says Maria. "I bet LeBron didn't even get good chunks of salt when he started out."

"I'll come to practice," says Victor. "But if we don't get any better, I'm outta there."

When he walks away, I say, "See? That's what a captain does."

CHAPTER 18

ON THE WALK HOME, I CAN'T HELP BUT think how some people just want to tear Creighton all the way down. They start with stealing our rec league players and then end up building a bunch of places with fancy food and super-expensive coffee.

In fact, as we're walking, I keep seeing signs up on telephone poles saying WE BUY UGLY HOUSES.

"What're all those signs?" I ask Ms. Estelle.

"People buy up old places," she says. "Then they fix them up or tear them down and build something fancier."

Well, what do they think is ugly? The houses here are old, but they ain't ugly.

C.J. suggests we head out to Kwik Spot, and I've got a craving for something crunchy myself, and enough change to buy a bit, so I go along. But when we step inside, this security guard guy says, "You-all got parents with you?"

"I got my grandmother," says Maria, nodding back toward Ms. Estelle.

"Gotta have one parent per student," says the guard. "And no backpacks."

"What, our money ain't no good here?" asks Maria.

Ms. Estelle starts arguing with the guy in Spanish. I don't know what they're saying, but he seems kinda embarrassed, and she seems super mad. But eventually, she says something to Maria, and Maria says, "Forget it."

I already know what the "no backpack" rule is. It means they think we're gonna steal. Bet they don't make that rule for every kid, though. Bet they don't have it at all the Kwik Spots on the North Side or out in the suburbs.

Ms. Estelle starts walking out, and we got no choice but to follow. She's mad when she gets out, still talking to Maria in Spanish. I only pick up a word here or there, but as we walk farther away, Maria explains it: He said we could only go in one at a time unless we all had parents. And no backpacks.

"They didn't have that rule before!" I said.

ARE THEY FOR REAL?
THEY THINK WE TRYNA STEAL?
WE'RE JUST LITTLE KIDS,
WE'D NEVER SKIP THE BILL.
WE PAY FOR WHAT WE GRAB

AND ALWAYS ENOUGH.
OR WE JUST PUT IT BACK
IF IT COSTS TOO MUCH.
I DON'T LIKE THIS RULE.
OUR BACKPACK...NO TAKIN' IT?
IT'S LIKE THEY'RE CALLIN' US THIEVES WITHOUT
ACTUALLY SAYIN' IT.

MR. WHEELER NEVER TRIPS IF THERE'S JUST
KIDS
BUT KWIK SPOT? I DON'T LIKE HOW THEY RUN
THEIR BIZ!

"Some new rule for after-school hours," she says. "My sister is gonna hit the roof when I tell her 'bout this."

"You know *that* never happens at Wheeler's," I say.

"I'll have my dad go in," says C.J. "He won't like this, either."

"But he can't fix it," says Maria. "This ain't like some corner store—that rule probably got made by people clear out in California or over in some whole other country. Kwik Spot is a big chain. They don't get to make their own rules all the time."

I wonder what Uncle Jamaal is gonna think of *that*.

The more I think about it, the more I'm on Mr. James's side. I know he don't like Kwik Spot. I like that they got so many snacks, and so cheap, but it's just…it don't feel like Creighton in there. If places are gonna start going out of business, that isn't worth it. I sure wouldn't trade Mr. Wheeler's for it. I *know* nobody at Kwik Spot is ever gonna give me an extra piece of gum for making up a rhyme.

In fact, the way things are going, I'll be lucky if they even let me in at all by the end of the school year!

Dad's getting out of his van just as I get home, and he seems like he's in a good mood. But I'm getting more and more worried. What if someone buys up Creighton Crest just to tear it down and build up one of those fifty-story high-rises? What if we get a bunch of new stores and they all start making up rules like at Kwik Spot?

"You okay, Simon?" Dad asks. "You seem kinda troubled."

"Is our rent going to go up?" I ask.

"Always goes up," he says, with a bit of a laugh. "That's what rent does. Every year."

"I mean, Mr. James was talking about gentrification," I said. "And I was thinking 'bout how Wheeler's was closed early, and there's all these signs up for people buying ugly houses...."

Dad sits down on the bumper of his van and motions for me to sit down by him.

"Mr. James is putting out some pretty advanced concepts for fifth grade," he says.

"We're not just students, we're scholars," I say.

"It's a tough issue for kids, though," he says. "Like, we all want them to start using nets instead of chains on the basketball hoops at the park. We want it to be safe for kids to go to the playground. But when it gets nicer, rent goes up. Would you believe this place has already gotten a lot better?"

"How?" I said. "Sunny's always talking about how it was a lot better when he was a kid."

"Old people always think that," says Dad,

laughing. "He was a kid in what, the 1950s? The kind of people putting up shops like Kwik Spot and that coffee shop wouldn't have *dreamed* of putting anything nice here back then. White people wouldn't even ride the bus through."

"Some of 'em still won't, right?" I say.

"Not as many. We got a ways to go, but it's gotten better here over the years. And they haven't kicked us out yet. I do get a bit worried about those 'we buy ugly houses' guys, though. Those guys can come in and just wreck a neighborhood sometimes. And I gotta admit, I'm worried about Wheeler's."

"We gotta do something," I say.

"You're playing for the Panthers," he says. "That's enough for a fifth grader."

"I gotta do more," I say. "This neighborhood is great, and people are forgetting. Maybe it's just cuz everybody been cooped up in their apartments for what feels like forever."

Dad pats me on the knee. "I'm sure you're going to think of something, Si. You always do."

Now, I don't normally watch the news much. But that night, while Dad is cooking up dinner, he's got it on. Aaron's watching it while he does his homework, and I'm sitting by him, showin' him the rhymes I'm working on for on the court. It sure doesn't feel like I'm a baby, watching the news.

On the TV people are talking about how they want people's pay to go up. And some people are saying it shouldn't. Like, this guy who says he's a real estate guy starts saying, "You think people flipping burgers should be making that much? You think barbers should be living in mansions? What next?"

"He better watch out," said Aaron. "If I was his barber, he'd get off the chair with the most ridiculous cut in history. Or no hair left at all!"

Why shouldn't barbers live in mansions? People respect barbers more than they respect guys like that!

TUESDAY

CHAPTER 19

THE NEXT DAY, I TRY TO COUNT ALL THE WE BUY UGLY HOUSES signs I see on the way to school. It's a lot. But joke's on them. Like I said, ain't no ugly houses around here! If people just take a bit more pride, they'll see how good it all is.

Before class even starts, when everyone is still acting a fool at their desks and blaming each other for cutting up, I walk up to Mr. James's desk.

"I think we got to do something."

He looks up and smiles. "Uh-oh," he says. "When the Notorious D.O.G. decides someone needs to do something, I know something's about to get done!"

"I was just thinking about what we've been talking about in social studies," I say. "I'm worried about Mr. Wheeler."

"I am, too, Simon."

"And Mr. Ray, and all those people who want to tear down the whole neighborhood. Did you see how many people came to watch the game on Friday?"

"Wasn't many," he said. "I think it was mostly parents."

"Not even every parent," I said. "Probably about as many people on the court as there were in the stands. And I don't get it. Every time I tell a grown person I'm playing for the Panthers, they start talking about how it's a Creighton tradition and I'm making Creighton proud, so you'd think they'd show up to a game."

"So how can we get 'em out to the next one?" he asks.

"I don't know. But we gotta do something," I say again.

"And I'm sure you'll think of something."

That's what Dad said, but I'm still not sure

what! I sit back down next to Maria and tell her all the stuff I've been talking about. And she says, "Pep rally!"

"What's a pep rally?"

"OM EM GEE, Simon. You ain't watching enough TV!" she says. "It's a thing high schools and stuff have before games. You get the whole school into the gym and get everybody all hype with school spirit and stuff. We could do one before the Panthers game, like a pep rally for the neighborhood."

That's not a bad idea! And even better—I get to tell Moms and Dad that someone thinks I'm not watching enough TV.

But I think I have seen that on TV. Before some big game, they drag everybody into the gym. Some kids complain about it, but everyone else is yelling and screaming, and then the cheerleaders come out, and all that. We could do that! We could get people all excited about the Panthers, and about Creighton. Moms was saying it's gonna be warmer this weekend, and one thing about it when you get those days where it's like forty-five degrees in January—everybody wanna come out and enjoy it while they can. We just gotta let 'em know that the game is on. And that it's free!

We don't have cheerleaders or anything like that, but I know we can come up with something. The Notorious D.O.G. has a plan!

CHAPTER 20

BOBBY AND VICTOR STILL AIN'T HANGING out much at recess. I never thought I'd say this, but I feel bad for Victor. When Bobby quit the team to go play for Garfield Park, it's like he quit the whole neighborhood. He walks around now like he's too good for Creighton. But at least when Victor gets a basketball, it's *us* he want to play with.

"You just need practice," he says. "All you can get. You're making *me* look bad out there!"

"Whatever," I say. "We all need it."

On the court, I practice blocking him and—just like Aaron said—using my rhymes to keep him distracted. While he's dribbling, I look right in his face and say, "Better think fast, or you ain't gonna last!" And in that second, while he's waiting to see what I'm gonna rhyme *fast* with, he's distracted, and I reach in and make the steal. It works!

And if it works on Victor, it's gonna work on other people, too.

The whole time we're playing, Mr. James is walking around talking to all the other teachers. He loved the idea of a pep rally and said we could use some class time that afternoon to start making flyers and that I could leave some of the stuff—like making sure we had the court at the rec center reserved early—all up to him.

I think he's actually hype to have something to do for the team besides passing out pretzels and saying stuff like "You miss every shot you don't take." Cuz here's the thing about Mr. James: He's not really a sports guy. He knows a lot about basketball *history*, but he's not the guy you'd ask to help you dribbling. But that don't matter, cuz he finds his own way to contribute.

If you think about it, it's just like being a

player on the team, right? Everyone has their own strengths and their own way of playing and their own thing that they bring to the table.

Like, on our team, Victor brings consistent skills. You can count on him to catch a pass and make a shot. C.J. brings all that, plus leadership. Everyone likes him. Janay brings the aggression. And me? I got the rhymes and the steals, and once I get the ball, no one's gonna be able to steal from me. All together, if we practice enough, I bet we could actually be a good team!

We're still playing when Bobby walks over.

"You ready to get your butts kicked this weekend?" he asks.

"Knock it off, Bobby," says Victor. "When you gonna give it a rest?"

"After we show you how a real team plays," he says. "You think you can ever get better playing with old flat basketballs that bounce like wet laundry? You get a ball that's actually inflated, you won't know what to do!"

"Just watch," I say. "We're gonna show you how we do it in Creighton Park!"

I sure hope that's right!

WEDNESDAY

CHAPTER 21

THE ONLY ONE *NOT* ALL HYPE ABOUT THE rally is C.J. Probably because Maria messed up and told him he should give a speech as captain of the team.

"I can't be giving speeches!" he says. "I wouldn't have been captain if I had to do THAT!"

"You knew captains gave the interviews," I said.

"Sure, but there weren't going to *be* any of them," he said.

"You make speeches lots," I say. "Like, when you told me to keep playing. That was a speech."

"Just to you, not to the whole neighborhood.

And what if I say something weird that no one thinks makes sense? Y'all don't mind when I do that, but the whole rest of Creighton?"

"Come on, C.J.," I say. "You also gave us that speech right before the game, remember? It made us all want to play."

"And look how that turned out!"

"C.J.," says Maria, "you don't *have* to make a speech. It'd just be nice, since it's a pep rally and all. You gotta embrace your inner leader."

"I've been trying to this whole time! Ain't I doing it?"

"You're doing it great," I say. "But aight, then. Don't worry about a speech. I'll be doing a rap, though. If I can rap, at least promise to think about it. Remember, this is for our hood!"

He told me his dad was pretty mad about how Kwik Spot wouldn't let us all in without parents. I can never guess what C.J.'s dad might get mad about. The way he usually talks, seems like he think gentrification would be a good thing. It's kinda like how in the fall, when people were protesting out in the streets, he thought it was all a waste of time.

But then, when we went to try to talk the city into fixing our air conditioners, he went with us and helped out.

Mr. James was saying he was gonna try to get local businesses involved. Like, have them selling stuff at the rally. Come be a part of it. I offered to talk to Mr. Wheeler myself. When I step into the door and the little bell goes *DING*, he smiles big.

"Rhymin' Simon!" he says. "Guess what? Got a fresh shipment of Duck Island Concord Grape in the cooler! And Maria, we got a few hot pickles in. I'll throw in a peppermint stick on the house."

"Thanks!" she says. She was gonna talk to him with me, but I guess the thought of having one of her gross pickles with a peppermint stick is too much. She runs right back to the hard candy.

I reach for a Concord Grape out of the cooler, and Mr. Wheeler asks me how the game was.

"We got beat pretty bad," I say. "And then you were closed. Is that...you know...Did you close because of the Kwik Spot?"

"Aw, don't you be worrying about that," he says. "I closed early so I could go to my granddaughter's violin recital, that's all. Nice thing about owning your own business. I can close up if I feel like it."

"Aren't you worried your rent might go up?"

"You don't gotta worry about me, young man. I'll worry about my prices, you worry about your grades and the next Panthers game!"

I'm glad to hear he's not in as much trouble as we thought, but who knows? Grown people never tell kids when they're in trouble. And it definitely can't hurt him to get some extra business.

"So, this Friday, before we play Garfield Park, we gonna have a whole pep rally at the rec center," I say. "Like, not just for the Panthers, but for Creighton Park. I was thinking, since you closed early... but if you were just closed to go to a recital, maybe you can't..."

"Rhymin' Simon, what did I just tell you about how I can close when I feel like it? You let me know what time, and I'll put a sign on the window telling people to come to the rec center instead of to the store, cuz that's where I'll be, selling all the hot pickles everybody could want!"

Yes!

I told him Mr. James would come by and set up all the details and stuff. Perfect! This is really gonna happen. We're gonna have the first ever Panthers Pep Rally, and then we gon' show them Wildcats how the *real* cats of Chicago get down! Go Panthers!

Outside, I bust into that Concord Grape. I don't know how a Concord grape is different from any other kind, but it sure makes the best kind of grape pop. Feels like forever since I had it. Knowing it came from Wheeler's makes it even better.

GOT THE BEST POP,
FINNA HAVE A PEP...
RALLY FOR THE SQUAD,
PANTHERS ARE THE BEST!
HOOD COMING THROUGH,
EVERYBODY REP!
IF THEY WAS SLEEPIN' ON US,
THEY'LL BE SORRY THAT THEY SLEPT!
WAKE UP! WAKE UP!
YEAH, MAKE IT LOUD!
FINNA DO IT BIG FOR THE CREIGHTON
PARK CROWD!

PICKLES, AND HOT CHIPS, AND POP ON DISPLAY,
THE PANTHERS GON' BRING IT TO CATS WHEN
WE PLAY!
WOOF WOOF!

I don't normally go into Mr. Ray's during the week, but this time we go next door, where he's giving a cut to some guy who looks like he's about two hundred years old. He's just finishing up, starting to rub in that stuff that makes your whole head feel like it's on fire. Aaron is already there, wearing his apron and cleaning up the mirrors, since there's not much hair to sweep.

I know Mr. Ray's gonna want to help. He's got pictures of all the Panthers teams from way back in the old days. For the first time, I notice he also got a picture of some old guy with long white hair and a mustache. That must be the barber Aaron was telling me about.

"Mr. Barnes," says Mr. Ray. "I thought you weren't due for a couple weeks."

"I'm not," I say. "I was just...well, we're having this pep rally on Friday before the Panthers play the Wildcats. Not just for the Panthers, like, for all of Creighton."

Maria steps in and tells him all about it, and Aaron listens while he wipes off a mirror.

"Mr. Wheeler's gonna come set up and sell refreshments and stuff," says Maria. "We know you've always supported the Panthers."

He laughs. "Well, just look at all the pictures on the wall! I got so many I can't keep 'em all up at once anymore. Gotta rotate. In fact, I might just have Aaron switch a few out. Those ones from the eighties, where the kids had the Jheri curl, ain't been up in too long."

"You got it, Mr. Ray," says Aaron. "Gotta get the year I was in back up, too. Scoring leader right here!"

Mr. Ray turns back to us. "I don't think they'd want me cutting hair in the rec center," he says as he slaps some more of that burning gunk on the old guy's head. "They'd probably worry I'd get some of this junk on their floor."

"They'd be right!" says the old guy. "That stuff'll burn right through. You think they need a tornado shelter? Cuz this stuff would make them one."

"Relax, Lester," says Mr. Ray. "You oughta be used to it by your age. Just be glad you have any hair left." Then he looks back at us and says, "And, anyway, Friday is a busy day for me here. But I bet I could offer up some coupons or something."

"I got it, Mr. Ray!" says Aaron. "I know what we could do."

"You hear this? Young man, five months on the job, hasn't even learned everyone's name yet, and he thinks he's got something." Mr. Ray laughs. "You young people amaze me."

"Don't you wanna hear it?"

"It's their pep rally. You kids wanna hear what Aaron thinks?"

"Gotta respect the scoring leader from back in the day," I say.

Aaron puts the cloth he was using to wipe mirrors down across the back of an empty chair.

"First of all," he says, "we gotta be using social media to get the word out. We want a whole crowd. People been cooped up too long with all this cold, and the pep rally's free...right?"

"Far as I know," I say. "Mr. James is probably handling that kinda stuff."

"Well, we'll get 'em all out there. Make sure they know it's a chance to show their Creighton pride, support local businesses, all that stuff. And then we give out a special prize."

"I can give out some coupons to start. People love getting a discount." Mr. Ray scratches his chin. "Then for the special prize, I can give a free haircut."

"But how 'bout this? Whoever wins the prize... gets to decide what kind of haircut you give Simon. Anything goes. Go bald, stripes...anything they decide," says Aaron.

Everybody but me starts laughing. I know where he got that idea! Just last night when we were watching the guy saying barbers didn't deserve mansions, and Aaron was thinking what the guy's barber could do to him.

Now he's thinking what someone could do to me!

For a second I panic.

What if I airball again, and they make me get some ridiculous cut to punish me?

But I gotta admit, it's a good idea.

And it's for Creighton.

It's gonna grow back, right?

"All right," I say. "I'll do it."

THURSDAY

CHAPTER 22

TURNS OUT THAT MR. JAMES HAS BEEN making the rounds! A lot of people in the neighborhood think the rally is a good idea. A couple of other businesses say they'll be on hand to sell stuff, and Uncle Jamaal even offers to help by making us *new uniforms*. He knows a guy who has something called a silk-screener, so when we turn up to practice on Thursday, there's a whole box of shiny blue Panthers jerseys waiting for us. They look almost like the ones pro players wear! None of the guys in the old pictures on Mr. Ray's wall got stuff like this on.

Between me and Maria, we got a bunch of posters and flyers stuck up all over the place. I made sure to cover those WE BUY UGLY HOUSES signs every chance I could. But it wasn't just us. C.J.'s sister Deijah made a few, but they're really just pictures. We posted those ones next to ones that have all the information and stuff.

Maria's sister Camille made a bunch, too, only Mr. James said we couldn't use all the ones she came up with. Some of them were about hating on Kwik Spot, and Mr. James said this is a pep rally. We're supposed to be celebrating the stuff we're proud of, not hating on anything.

"We just won't talk about Kwik Spot at all," he says.

So it's all coming together. Except for two things.

One is that I'm getting nervous. What if somebody like Bobby gets to pick my new hairstyle? At dinner I said Aaron should have volunteered himself to be the one getting whatever haircut someone wants, and he said, "I got my rep to think about."

And just like clockwork, Moms and Dad said,

"You're only fifteen, you don't have a rep yet." Then they laughed like crazy. I think it's from an old song. One of their rap oldies, I guess.

So now, at practice, we're talking a lot about it.

"Everybody's gonna be hype by the rally," says Coach Thomas. "Now, we don't have to be perfect. We just have to play with everything we've got and show them they've got something to be proud of."

"We already know they do!" Mr. James adds. "But every time they cheer for you, they'll be cheering for our neighborhood, too."

So, Coach Thomas works with us. I show her what Aaron taught me about dribbling and stealing, and she gives me a few pointers that help even more.

"You're gonna be unstoppable one of these days, Simon," she says. "Keep working at it. You're gonna be like a secret weapon. People relax and think they got it easy when they're going up against a short basketball player. Are they right?"

"No, Coach!" Then I drop one of my rhymes: *"I may not be B-I-G, but I'm the Notorious D.O.G.!"*

I told Mr. James about the rhyming thing that Aaron told me about. He didn't seem all that happy about it at first, but he came around.

"You know the kids on the other teams are gonna trash-talk," Coach Thomas tells him. "This way, he can give it back and not be disrespectful. You said he was a good rapper, right?"

"That's true," he says.

"That's what it's all about," she says. "Playing to each player's strengths."

Mr. James still made me show him all the rhymes I was coming up with to use on the court, just to make sure none of them are bad. He said they could be cheesy—can't prevent a steal when you're busy groaning at a cheesy rhyme—but nothing mean.

It's still pretty exciting, though. It's like me and Aaron invented a whole new version of trash-talking!

By the end of practice, I feel like I'm seeing a real difference. For one thing, the kids who usually goof off are pretty hype that we might have a crowd to watch us, so they play a lot harder. And the plays Coach is coming up with are working! Some of them I don't understand at first, but C.J. can usually explain it to me.

I'm starting to think we might actually, just maybe, have a chance to win this game! Bobby and Louis ain't gon' know what hit 'em!

FRiDAY

CHAPTER 23

LAST NIGHT, I HAD A CRAZY DREAM.

I dreamt that I showed up for the pep rally, only no one was there! Not even all the players on the team. All the Wildcats, but not enough Panthers to even cover every position.

And the crowd for the pep rally? Nothing but Moms, Dad, my brothers, and that real estate guy from TV the other night.

But I still went up to do my rap, but then I just froze. I forgot every line!

And instead of making a speech, C.J. decided

he didn't want to be captain anymore. Or even a Panther.

But after we talked, I got him to agree to play out this one last game, just because the real estate developer was watching, and if we lost, he was gon' buy up the Creighton Crest apartment building to tear it down, and replace Wheeler's store with a fancy nightclub, and Mr. Ray's with a place where tacos cost a hundred dollars.

So we played, but we got our butts kicked, and Bobby was dropping rhymes on *me*!

When the final buzzer came off the scoreboard, the real estate guy laughed and showed off the picture of the big glass high-rise building he's gonna put where Creighton Crest was. Then Dad said we wouldn't be able to afford it anymore and we'd have to move to Indiana.

And then he said he won a prize to pick my haircut, and he was gonna make me get a cut like that clown in the fire safety video they show us every year, and with some special chemical that means my hair'll never go back to normal.

☆ ☆ ☆

After I finally wake up, I lie there for a while, thinking about how sad I am that we have to move, and most of all, how sad it was that no one even came to the big pep rally. It takes a few minutes before I realize that none of it really happened. You ever have that? One time I dreamed I forgot to turn in a work sheet in second grade, so they were sending me all the way back to kindergarten. I woke up and tried to work out how old I'd be when I graduated. I was out of bed before I remembered that it was just a dream, and I really *did* finish second grade!

This time, though, it's kinda harder to shake.

The rally hasn't happened yet! Maybe no one *will* show up!

And maybe all that stuff with the real estate guy... Mr. James talked about that happening in other neighborhoods. Could that still happen here?

Also, I keep touching my hair, making sure it's still there.

At least I don't look like a clown yet!

☆ ☆ ☆

All through breakfast, I can't shake that feeling from the dream. But when I finally open the door to head to school, the sun is out and you can actually *feel* it, and that kinda pushes the dream out of my head. If it was still September or something we'd all prolly say it was freezing, but after the last few weeks, with all the snow and the Polar Vortex and everything, it feels like the whole city is coming back to life.

And everybody else seems to think so, too. The last few weeks, when you passed somebody else at all, waiting on the bus or whatever, they were all bundled up and didn't even look at you. This morning, a lot more people are out, crowding into the streets. And every block or two, we meet someone we know, and all of them ask me about the rally.

I know there's some more swag in my step, cuz I feel a hundred pounds lighter without all them layers on.

"What are you *doing*?" asks Maria.

"I'm dancing!"

She busts out laughing. "OH EM GEE! You look like somebody poured fire ants down your shirt!"

I know I kinda look a mess. I've been doing so many basketball moves it's like my body can't remember how to do dancing moves. Plus it's been a day longer than I usually go between shape-ups at Mr. Ray's, but that's the point. By dinnertime, I might not have any hair at all!

CHAPTER 24

AT SCHOOL, MR. JAMES BRINGS MRS. LEARY and her whole class into our room so we can all make signs for people to hold at the pep rally. Everybody's getting into it. Aaron's been spreading the word on the internet, and people are really hype to come see us play.

"Give me that marker!"

"Y'all got the blue paint?"

"Watch the floor!"

It's really something to watch. All over the room, people are making a mess. All cuz Maria and I had some idea to have a pep rally!

While we work, Mr. James is going over the program. A couple of girls who do step dance volunteered to do a routine, and Maria and her debate team friends came up with a couple of cheers.

"Coach Thomas will introduce the team," says Mr. James. "And I'll give a talk about what we've been talking about here in class, about neighborhoods and gentrification. Simon, how's your rap coming?"

"I got it about written," I say.

I might be stretching the truth a little bit there. I've got a few lines written, but so far I keep writing a few, then throwing them out. I want this one to be perfect.

I guess I better hurry.

"Good. And C.J., you know the captain's gotta talk to everybody."

C.J. just kinda looks around the room, like he didn't hear. Maybe he didn't.

"I've got a speech written for him!" says Maria. She shows it to Mr. James, and he smiles, then asks C.J. to come and read it.

He moves his head around a bit, like he isn't liking it. Like the face he makes when he's getting crushed on Fortnite and he knows it.

"I kinda like this stuff about how we're different from other places, cuz we got heart," he says. "But you know that every other neighborhood probably says that, too."

"I sure hope so," says Mr. James.

"Plus, it just don't sound like something I'd say," he says. "I'll try. I can't promise I'll get it. But I'm gonna try."

"That's all I ask," says Mr. James.

All the stuff going on in the room—all the yelling and painting and everything happening at once—isn't really the sort of scene he vibes in. And Mr. James knows it. He might not be C.J.'s teacher, but he knows what's up.

"Tell ya what," he says. "You want to go work on a speech back in Mrs. Leary's room? You can even put on headphones."

"Yeah!"

See, I would never want to miss out on what was happening in Mr. James's room. It's almost like a party. Sometimes I come up with rhymes so fast that I gotta write 'em down before I forget 'em. But C.J. doesn't work like that.

Only one person don't look happy, and that's Bobby.

"Come on," Victor says. "This still your neighborhood, even if you went to play for somebody else."

"I don't see you making posters for Garfield Park," says Bobby.

"You switched teams, so what?" says Victor. "Just cuz you switched teams don't mean you switched neighborhoods, or that you had to switch friends."

"Yeah," says Kenny. "When you gonna get over that? You weren't on the same soccer team last spring, and you were still friends."

"I guess," says Bobby.

"And anyway," says Maria, "you want your parents' rent to go up, so you have to move so far away you can't even get to Garfield Park anymore? You might end up living in Indiana!"

Bobby thinks for a minute, then he grabs a marker and some poster board.

He doesn't make any signs that say anything about the Panthers, but I guess that's fair enough. He just draws pictures of basketballs and jerseys. Mr. James tells him he can make one for the Wildcats, if he wants. Garfield Park people deserve to be proud even if this is a Creighton pep rally.

"When our neighbors are strong, it makes us all stronger," he says.

By the end of the day, we got tons of posters. Mr. James uses the SMART Board to show all the social media stuff Aaron came up with.

"And look how many responses he got! This is gonna be like a winter version of a block party. It's just what everybody needs."

"All we really need," says Maria, "is to win the game!"

CHAPTER 25

BY THE TIME WE GET INTO THE REC CENTER it's like the whole world explodes. There are already a whole bunch of people out in the bleachers, cheering for us!

The rally ain't even started yet, but Mr. James is working the crowd, greeting the people who walk in, shouting out people in the stands, and reading out the signs. Maria and Camille are by the door, passing them out to people to wave around.

This is lit, and it ain't even started.

There's still a game to think about, so I put my coat and my hoodie away, then go over to the corner where the rest of the team is warming up. C.J. and I pass a ball back and forth. I try to do that move spinning a ball on my finger, like Maria can, but I'm not very good at it. Not yet, anyway!

Coach Thomas goes back and forth from helping Mr. James to helping us.

Off to the side, Mr. Wheeler has a table set up with drinks, snacks, and stuff like that. He knows everybody, and it seems like he already knows what people want before they even order. Looks like he's making some bank, too, which is good.

Over on the corner, I see Bobby getting all distracted. He should be warming up. Now and then he spins the ball on his finger, like he trying to get attention, but people just ignore him. All this coulda been for him, too.

The official pep rally starts by having the couple of girls from Mrs. Leary's class do their stepping, then Maria and her friends do their cheer.

Mr. James is on the microphone, which is a dangerous thing. You give Mr. James a microphone, you might not ever get it back! People cheer for him so loud he has to do his hand thing to calm them down.

Once the crowd is settled, Mr. James gets all serious, talking about stuff like the alderman and zoning ordinances. To tell you the truth, stuff that kinda goes over my head. But grown-ups clap and shout things like "I know that's right!"

"Anyway," he says, "this is what we've been talking about in my class. We all want our neighborhood to be the best it can be. We want them to fill in all those empty storefronts, fix all the broken lights, get us all the funding we need for the programs in the schools. But we also don't want people to drive up our rents and drive us out. And no one's ever quite figured out how to make both of those things work, but we can start by supporting people like Mr. Wheeler, Mr. Ray, Sal's Sandwiches, and the Chicago Corner!"

People clap more with each local business he mentions. You can tell they're feeling the Creighton Park pride. Mr. Wheeler catches me looking at him and tosses a piece of gum over at me. I can't go around chewing on gum right when a game's about to start, but I get it. He's glad.

"And now," says Mr. James, "let me bring out a young man who really put his foot into this pep rally. He was the one who came to me and said we had to do something, and now he's gonna come up and rap for you a bit. Creighton's own Notorious D.O.G., Simon Barnes!"

People clap when they hear my name!

I gotta tell you, that's something I could really get used to. Once I'm the super-famous Notorious D.O.G., it'll happen all the time, right? Probably won't usually be for playing basketball, though! I've gotten a lot better, but I know that still ain't what I'm gonna be famous for.

Today, though, I'm Simon, a Panthers basketball player.

And I feel like I could slam-dunk without even needing a trampoline. Or needing to cut one to lift off the ground, like Kenny says. I could just float it on up.

"Y'all ready for this?" shouts Mr. James as I walk up to him. "I don't think y'all are ready for this!"

"I think they're ready," I say. "I mean, I trust them."

"Before he starts," says Mr. James, "we gotta tell you about the contest. On the way in, each of you got a ticket with a number on it. After the game, we're going to add up all the points on each side, and whoever got that number on your ticket... you all see how Simon here could use a shape-up? Well, we're gonna walk down to Mr. Ray's, and the winner gets to pick what kind of haircut he gets!"

People laugh, making me nervous, and Mr. James rubs it in. "Now, if I won, I'd just get him a nice, proper haircut. But you might think he looks better with one of those punk rock looks, with pink hair... maybe just some spikes... he's willing to risk it all! I told you, this young man is putting his foot in this pep rally!"

I don't know about pink hair, but I can't let them see my nerves getting all rattled. I pretty much have to reach out and grab the mic from Mr. James, but that's how it is. You give him a mic, you gotta be hype to get it away from him. And I gotta start rapping before he gives whoever wins the contest any more ideas!

It's a lot of people watching me.

And for a second all that feeling of the nightmare comes back.

But then, the second I put the mic up to my mouth, it all melts away, and I let it go:

LET'S GET IT GOIN', EVERYBODY GET HYPE!
TONIGHT IS THE NIGHT, AND WE READY FOR A FIGHT!
WE GON' MAKE THE WILDCATS RUN AWAY IN FEAR
CUZ THE REAL CATS, THE CREIGHTON PARK PANTHERS, ARE HERE!

WE ALL KNOW THAT THIS THE BEST PLACE AROUND,
THE DOPEST NEIGHBORHOOD IN THE WHOLE CHI-TOWN!
WE PANTHERS GOT PRIDE, PROUD OF WHERE WE STAY,
GONNA SHOW IT ALL OFF TONIGHT WHEN WE PLAY!

SHOUT OUT MR. RAY, FOR CUTTIN' HAIR HERE FOR YEARS,

SO EVERY TIME WE SCORE, Y'ALL SHOULD GIVE
HIM A CHEER!
SHOUT OUT MR. WHEELER, FOR HAVING A COOL
STORE,
CELEBRATE HIS WORK EVERY TIME THE
PANTHERS SCORE!

WE ABSOLUTELY LOVE LIVING HERE IN
CREIGHTON PARK.
THE KIDS AND FAMILIES WHO GOT A LOTTA
HEART!
SO PANTHERS, COACH T, MR. JAMES?!
WE ALL READY NOW, LET'S GET IN THE GAME!
WOOF WOOF!
NOTORIOUS D.O.G.! THAT'S ME!

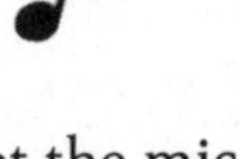

Mr. James is coming up to get the mic back, but I ain't done. And I gotta move fast if I want to keep him from getting it back.

"Now, everybody," I say, "we gotta get this game on, so let me bring out the captain of the Panthers, C.J.!"

C.J. is behind me, standing there, looking off at nothing. But when people cheer, he turns, and then his face breaks into a smile. Like in the movie where the pirate's just been captured but he knows something the people capturing him don't.

"Thanks, Simon," he says. "Uh…I'm C.J. And the other day this other store told me I couldn't have my backpack, like I was gonna steal. But Mr. Wheeler, he never does that. And I might not be able to get as many Flamin' Hots from him as I could at some other store, but I know when I buy from him, that money stays in Creighton Park instead of going to some guy who ain't ever even been here. When we buy in Creighton, Creighton wins. Y'all ready to see Creighton win today?"

Everyone cheers, and then C.J. laughs. "Well, if you wanna see Creighton win, a Panthers game ain't usually the best place to go, but you're about to see us give a hundred and ten percent, take all the shots we can, make our attitude everything, and not prepare to fail."

When he's done, he turns to me, all smiling. He's actually liking this captain thing! I knew he would. Sometimes with C.J., you just gotta help him figure out he can do something. He always thinks he can't at first. But we all know better.

Coach Thomas takes the mic and gives this nice speech about how she's seen us all improve so much in such a short time.

And then we clear off the microphone, C.J. shakes hands with the Wildcats captain, and it's time for the game.

I'm feeling fly, and I'm *ready* to fly.

CHAPTER 26

FIRST TIME I'M GOING ONE-ON-ONE WITH A guy on the court, he's dribbling, and I say, *"Better not be hatin' if you're coming to Creighton!"* and make the steal.

I made it!

I dribble a few times, running right by him, and pass it to Janay, who aims at the backboard and misses, but C.J. makes it on the rebound.

Score!

But then the Wildcats get a fast break down to the other end of the court, and before I even know what's happening, they got the ball in the basket.

C.J. manages to get the ball, and I get in front of a guy who's tryna get in his way. He reaches up, like shooting a skyhook shot, and gets it up over the guys who are trying to block him. The ball doesn't go in, but it doesn't get knocked down, which feels like a win to me, personally.

Only, you know, not as much of a win as if we were actually winning. Pretty soon the Wildcats have pushed it down the court and sunk another one.

Sometimes it seems like they're moving like lightning. Score, score, score. These guys are good. They move like magic—not air-ball magic, but real magic—and the ball just keeps going up and up and up. We've been practicing against each other, not against people like this. But now and then, I get ahold of the ball. Just like I practiced. While some tall girl's dribbling, I can smack the ball and move. And, if possible, get it to C.J.

Because once C.J. finally gets his hands on the ball, he and Victor are on fire. They pass it between them so fast it's a blur. But when C.J. goes to make the shot, Bobby gets the steal. Except I'm right there with another rhyme: *"I may not be tall, but I can still get this ball!"* and *yoink!* Take that, Bobby! I shoot, and *swish!* Another point for the Panthers!

Everything is coming together and it seems like nothing can take us down.

By the end of the first half, the Panthers are up by one. We're up! We're winning! They're faster than us, probably taller than us, and have more really good players than we do, but we're not just holding our own, we're staying ahead!

The crowd is so loud the whole place is shaking. Maria and her friends run out and do a cheer:

STAND UP,
IT'S TIME TO SHOUT!
COME ON FANS,
YELL IT OUT!
SAY IT LOUD!
SAY IT PROUD!
LET'S GO PANTHERS! GET THAT BALL!

Everybody is stomping and yelling, and let me tell you, I feel like a million bucks and nothing can beat it. (Except maybe a sick rhyme.)

C.J. pulls us into a huddle. "I don't have much to say except keep doing what you're doing!"

We clap hands and yell, "Go, Panthers!" before we run back onto the court.

At the beginning of this quarter, the Wildcats get the ball. Bobby shoots and *BONK*. Brick! C.J. snatches that ball and runs as fast as he can. Passes it to Janay, who shoots, and *swish!* YES!

The Panthers are UNSTOPPABLE!

Or, anyway, it seems like it for a minute.

I'm running so hard I'm sweating out a whole swimming pool. By the time the second half is coming down, my feet are hurting. And I've only made a couple of shots on my own. But scoring isn't my department—mine is to get the ball to C.J. and distract people who are trying to stop him, or trying to make a shot on their own. And it's working! If I hadn't made a couple of steals and dropped a couple of rhymes that got people's mind off the game long enough for us to take advantage, it'd be a total loss. C.J. is definitely the best, but he's not doing it all by himself.

And when the buzzer goes off, the score is tied. Tied!

1
25
PANTHERS
2

But Bobby got fouled on the last shot, so the Wildcats get to shoot free throws. If Bobby makes just one out of the two shots, that's it. If he misses, we get some overtime, and we've still got a shot.

C.J. pulls us into another huddle. "Look. We can't do anything right now but watch and hope for the best. No matter what, we played a good game tonight."

C.J. might think all is lost, but I still have a couple things up my sleeve.

We all line up in the paint, and Bobby dribbles a bit at the line. While he does, I turn back to the crowd and start chanting, "Creighton! Creighton!"

It doesn't take much. Maria starts shouting it, too, and then pretty soon everyone's chanting and stomping their feet. No way Bobby can keep his concentration.

"You hear that, Bobby?" I call out. "They're reminding you who you're letting down by playing for the Wildcats."

He gives me a look, then shoots the ball.

Air ball!

He shot an air ball!

Oh man, after all the times he got on me for it, he airballs right during a free throw!

The crowd starts doing the "air ball" thing, right on key. Mr. James waves his arms to stop them, even though it's magic and it's the other team. And I get it. It's not, you know, classy. Whole point of today is to show that Creighton has *class*, right?

One more shot.

I turn back and just shout "Creighton!" again. I don't know how there's even still sweat left in my body after all that game, but I'm dripping.

"You hear Creighton calling, Bobby?" I ask. "Creighton's the best, you know it's true. You ain't never getting that ball through!"

He dribbles one more time and takes the shot.

Swish.

CHAPTER 27

WELL, LIKE C.J. SAID, IF YOU WANNA SEE Creighton win, a Panthers game is not really the place you should go.

But we didn't lose anywhere near as bad as we did that first game, and the Wildcats are a better team than the Tornadoes. All the stuff Coach Thomas taught us is paying off. Few more games like this, and we might even start winning.

And no one seems mad that we lost, either. The crowd is still cheering, especially after Mr. James announces the total of both scores, and the winning ticket is Deijah! C.J.'s sister!

She gives me this evil grin, like the kind girls her age give you in movies when they know a monster's about to jump out the TV or something, but I barely even notice. Everybody's patting me on the back. Moms, Dad, Markus, and DeShawn. Uncle Jamaal comes over and daps me up. Mr. James tells me how proud he is of me. Mr. Wheeler hands me over a frosty-cold bottle of Duck Island Concord Grape.

I sure don't *feel* like I just lost.

Markus and DeShawn even pick me up on their shoulders, and we start walking down to Mr. Ray's.

"Watch out!" I say. "There's still some ice on the edge of the sidewalk! Y'all drop me, Moms'll never let you forget it."

"Just relax and enjoy the view," says DeShawn. "Shorty finally gets to see what the world looks like to everybody who's regular-sized!"

Ha. Ha.

When they put me down outside the store, Maria is standing by me. "You ain't *got* to do this, you know," she says. "You want me to talk to Deijah and talk her into just giving you a regular shape-up?"

I shake my head. "Kinda do. But I made this deal for Creighton."

Once we step in, with my family plus a whole crowd of people from the pep rally behind us, Mr. Ray tells the old guy he's cutting on to get up off the chair. "I'll finish you later," he says. "Right now we got some business."

The old man looks mad at first, but then he sees something's up and he calms down some. It's Mr. Ray's place, he makes the rules, and everybody knows it.

"Who's the lucky winner?" asks Mr. Ray.

"Me!" shouts Deijah. Mr. Ray laughs and shakes his head at me. "All right, Mr. Barnes. Hop up and meet your fate."

I get in the chair. My armpits are getting real moist but can't let anybody see the Notorious D.O.G. sweat. Plus I'm still feeling so good, it covers up every other feeling.

The seat's warm from the old guy's butt, which is kinda gross. But that's overshadowed, too.

"All right, Deijah. What's it gonna be?"

She smiles and says, "It can be anything I want?"

"I believe that was the rule."

"Give him a normal shape-up, but then one bald stripe, right down the middle!"

I groan, but I laugh, too.

And when he finishes, I look in the mirror, and you know what?

It looks cool.

It looks... Notorious!

WHAT?

YUP!

LOOK AT THAT HAIRCUT!

I THOUGHT IT'D BE TOO MUCH

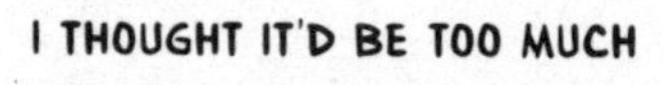

BUT YEAH, IT'S JUST ENOUGH!

A BALD STRIPE DOWN THE MIDDLE'S SO FUN-NY!

I LOOK LIKE MOSES PARTING THE RED SEA!

DEIJAH DID HER BEST, AND ACTUALLY, IT AIN'T THE WORST!

MAYBE I'LL START A NEW STYLE AND BE THE FIRST.

NAH, THAT WON'T HAPPEN, WHO AM I KIDDING?

BUT I'M STILL PROUD OF MYSELF FOR NOT
QUITTING!

I DIDN'T QUIT THE PANTHERS, AND NOT
CREIGHTON PARK

AND NOW MY REWARD IS A CUT WITH A PART!

BUT IT'S FOR A GOOD CAUSE, SO ME, I'M
NOT MAD.

SIMON WITH A STRIPE DOESN'T LOOK SO BAD!

ONE MONTH LATER

THE POLAR VORTEX IS FINALLY GONE FOR real, and I'm glad I can walk outside without the wind freezing my boogers. It sure is easy to take breathing for granted until it hurts to do it. It's actually nice for this time of year (if you can call forty-five degrees nice), and there's all kinds of people out today. And my jacket is unzipped, so everybody can see my Panthers jersey.

C.J. is dribbling a basketball while we walk, but then he stops to sneeze. Maria sneaks up and snatches the ball right from him.

"Aw, that ain't fair!" groans C.J. "My eyes were closed."

"And I saw an opportunity and took it." Maria spins the ball on her finger. "I guess all your captain talk motivated me!"

"Does this mean you'll be on the team with us next year?" I ask.

She shakes her head. "Naw. Even C.J. can't talk me into giving up debate. But I can still kick your butt at recess!"

Real talk: It wouldn't be that hard. Today is the last game of the season and we are 0 and 7. But at least we're not getting our fundaments kicked as bad as when we first started. Last week we only lost by three points. Maybe we can pull off a win today!

But first we stop at Wheeler's. It's a big day for him and I have a special rap all ready.

"I'm glad we're here. I'ma need me some Flamin' Hots to get fired up!" C.J. says loudly. If you ask me, he's plenty fired up already, but I ain't gonna be the one to tell him to chill.

It's crowded in Wheeler's. It's been like this ever

since the pep rally, but today it's way more crowded than usual. The whole neighborhood is in here! And Mr. Wheeler is grinning so big it's a wonder his cheeks aren't hurting him. "Rhymin' Simon! Excuse me, the Notorious D.O.G.! Just in time!"

"That's right," I say.

He tosses me a piece of gum. "For luck!"

"Thanks!"

HEY, MR. WHEELER, MR. BIG DEAL-ER,
THE BIG MAN IN CHARGE, NOW YOUR STORE'S
GETTIN' LARGE!
BIGGER THAN A MANSION, IT'S CALLED AN
EXPANSION,
GETTIN' A MAKEOVER, MAKE IT PRETTY, MAKE IT
HANDSOME!
ALL KINDS OF PEOPLE MEANS ALL KINDS OF
SALES
AND ALL OF THOSE SALES MEANS YOU'RE
PROBABLY DOING SWELL!
THAT'S HOW IT SHOULD BE, CUZ YOU'RE A PART
OF CREIGHTON.
THE STORE MAKES A DIFFERENCE, SO MONEY'S
WHAT YA MAKIN'!

I'MA GET MY CONCORD GRAPE IN THIS SHOP,
AND C.J. GON' ALWAYS GET HIS HANDS ON
FLAMIN' HOTS.
MARIA'S GOT THE PICKLES, AND WE ALL
COMIN' IN,
TOGETHER AS COMMUNITY, AS FAMILY, AS
FRIENDS!
THAT'S THE WAY IT'S BEEN, AND THE WAY IT'S
GONNA BE!
AND SOMETIMES, I'LL EVEN GET A STICK OF GUM
FOR FREE!
GOOD OL' MR. WHEELER'S, EVERYBODY GIVE A
CHEER!
A CREIGHTON PARK SPECIAL, AND WE'RE HAPPY
THAT IT'S HERE!

When I'm done, people cheer real loud. This feeling won't ever get old.

Turns out people don't like feeling like they don't belong in a store where they're spending money, so some of us gave up on Kwik Spot real fast. Some of us made their way back to Wheeler's and his hot pickles and bubble gum and Concord Grape pop. But I also think those people made their way back to the way it feels in here. Like a warm hug that can erase the sting from every Polar Vortex.

Everybody is talking and laughing and picking out their favorite things. Maria runs to the candy aisle for her peppermint stick and C.J. goes to get his Cheetos.

The cash register ain't stopped cha-chinging yet.

"We need to get going," C.J. says after he pays. "Tip-off is in an hour!"

"Creighton Park Panthers, LET'S GO!" yells Maria, and everybody starts yelling with her. Yeah, you would never get this at a Kwik Spot. And I wouldn't trade it for all the Concord Grape in the world.

As soon as we step outside, Mr. Ray pokes his head out the door of the barbershop. "Come on in here. I wanna show y'all something!"

"Aw, Mr. Ray, we gon' be late to warm-ups if we stop now," C.J. says. "It's our last game of the season!" This is how I know C.J. is really into being captain. He ain't never talked back to Mr. Ray!

"Boy, don't you think I know that? This ain't gon' take but a minute."

C.J. and I look at each other. I shrug and follow Mr. Ray inside. He takes us right to the wall with all the pictures of the teams. And there we are, right in the middle, with our blue jerseys and my fresh haircut.

"That's real dope, Mr. Ray," I say.

"Y'all are a part of Creighton Park history," he says, "and I'm real proud of both of you. This is the least I can do."

"Thanks, Mr. Ray!"

"My pleasure. Now get on outta here. You got a game to play!"

And just like always, the Panthers are getting our fundaments kicked bad! Like, extra bad! We ain't never lost by eighteen points!

The party at Mr. Wheeler's pretty much followed us to the rec center, so today the crowd is bigger than ever. I like that the community is all together but you would think all that extra noise would give us an edge. Instead it makes me kinda squirmy and makes my hands slippery.

Oh well. It doesn't bother me as much anymore (well, maybe a little bit), because we have a lot of fun playing. Ever since C.J. gave his big speech at the pep rally, I just keep focusing on getting better instead of winning. And it feels good!

And since we're losing so bad, ain't no point in getting all worked up and taking everything extra serious. That's part of why we're losing so bad. But we're having a good time. Up until I get fouled on the last play!

Making these baskets won't even make a difference, but you know what? I'm not throwin' away my shot.

Maria's voice comes loud from the bleachers. "OH EM GEE! You got this, Simon!"

And then like magic, *everybody* is cheering me on.

LAST SHOTS OF THE GAME, WILL I MAKE THEM
OR MISS?
IT'S ALL JUST FUN, BUT I HOPE I CAN SWISH!
WE AIN'T GONNA WIN, BUT THAT PART DOESN'T
MATTER
CUZ I'M A CREIGHTON PARK PANTHER AND A
REALLY DOPE RAPPER!
BEEN RHYMIN' ON THE COURT, MAKE POINTS
AND STEALS.
ALL SEASON, EACH OF US BEEN SHOWIN' OFF
OUR SKILLS.
IF I MAKE 'EM OR MISS, IT'S ALL GOOD, YOU SEE
CUZ I'M SIMON, THE NOTORIOUS D.O.G.
WOOF WOOF!

I line up the first shot, and *swish!* Nothing but net! YES!

I line up for the second shot and I don't come anywhere near close.

And then right on cue, they all turn on me.

"Air ballllllll!"

And that magic Maria is always talking about? With all the harmonies and all that? Here it is again. It really is something special, even if it's because I did end up throwing away my shot. Again. But it don't seem like that big of a deal anymore and I just shrug and laugh, then I join in the chorus.

"Air balllll!"

There's another kind of magic, too. The whole neighborhood is clowning on me together, but this same neighborhood saved Wheeler's store. They are here cheering for us even though we ain't that great. And that's what makes Creighton Park so special. As long as we stick together like this, we'll always be winners, no matter what the scoreboard says.

ACKNOWLEDGMENTS

Moms, you're the MVP and you've always been that to me. As kids, we used to hate when you'd take us to the library and we'd stay there for hours, but I guess it paid off, right? Your little boy has a book on shelves that real-life people can choose to buy. Praise Jesus! Would you ever have thought? I'm sure your answer is "Uh, yeah—cuz you're *my* son." Well, here we are, and it only happened because of you. Thanks for being so gracious with me and loving me even when I didn't see what you saw. Now you can take your grandkids to the library or to the bookstore to check this one out! And you know what? I'll even see if I can get the author to sign it for them—just because I love you. Keep being a trooper. Love, Mookie.

Dionté, your love for reading has always inspired

me. The reason I started reading more is because I once saw you with a book that had hundreds of pages and knew I couldn't let you show me up. So, I went and got two books with hundreds of pages, and the rest is sibling-rivalry history! I'll let you think you're a better reader than me if you promise to take a look at this one in your spare time. Wait—never mind—you'll never be that, but you'll always be my big, little brother! I love you, dude.

DeJhari, you're the best sister I've ever had. To date, lovingly helping raise you alongside Mommy has been one of my greatest accomplishments. I feel honored to be your brother, and to be honest, I think you're one of the biggest reasons why I love kids. I remember when you suggested that we start our own book club. It was such an awesome idea, and hearing you break down literature with such ease was absolutely beautiful. Your mind, your talent, your humor, your thoughtfulness, and your care for others are all tremendous things, and I can't wait to see how you continue to use who you are to help make the world a better place. I love you, Jhari.

Dear Nana and Papa, thank you for being awesome grandparents. Nana, you taught me how to read. 'Nuff said. Game changer. You win. But also, thanks for letting me take all those naps at your house and for singing "In the Name of Jesus" to me. It was comforting. You have always been my comfort. You're definitely my #1 Nana. And Papa, thank you for helping me to T-H-I-N-K. You've always been so careful and thoughtful with everything, and thankfully, I think those traits have been passed down to me. Thank you for letting me grow up in the house you built. I love you both.

Elizabeth, you are such a G! I know you do this literary agent stuff for a bunch of people, but you've made me feel like I'm your only client. I don't feel like I'm just any random ol' author with you; I feel like THE author with you! You make this feeling happen. Thank you for taking a shot on a kid from Chicago who didn't know nothin' about nothin'. And thank you for always challenging me and fighting for me. You should be proud of your work, EB. Thank you.

Sam, from the moment we spoke together on

the phone that first time, I *knew* I was going to publish with you and Little, Brown. You believed in Simon, and I felt that energy from you immediately. In fact, I literally only chose Little, Brown Books for Young Readers because of you. You have been one of the most gracious and sweetest editors during this whole process, and I wish you nothing but success and happiness moving forward. Thank you, Sam.

Ronni, thank you for being a shining star and helping me shine my light brighter to the world. You've helped bring Simon to life and I will forever be grateful to you.

Shout-out to all the kids on the West Side of Chicago. Y'all are some of the brightest, funniest, most beautiful people in the entire world. Don't ever let anybody tell you what you can't do. Put on for y'all's city, man. I love you to bits and pieces.

Dear Chaseton and Cambridge, thank you both for changing my everything. You two being here has redeemed so much in my life. I can't wait to see you all reading books like Simon and many others. Maybe y'all will even rap like your pops one day.

Whatever you do, you'll both be great. Daddy loves you so much.

Dear Simoné, a full book couldn't completely capture what I feel for you. I have loved you since we were Simon's age, and I will love you until the last chapter of our life is complete. Thank you for being my everything, Monie. Love, Dwaynie Pooh.